KT-145-076

Granny Nothing
and the Secret Weapon

Polly suddenly jumped on Elvis, taking him completely by surprise. She started battering him with her schoolbag. Presley saw what was happening and tried to leap over the school gates to get in to help Elvis. He dragged Nanny Sue behind him. She was caught on the gates, screaming for help.

The assembly hall went wild. Polly and Elvis were locked in mortal combat. Presley was careering back and forth past the window dragging a screaming Nanny Sue behind him.

Total chaos.

Pandemonium.

But just another ordinary day in the life of the McAllisters.

Have you read the other books in this weird,
wonderful, wobbly series?

Granny Nothing

Granny Nothing and the Shrunken Head

Granny Nothing and the Rusty Key

Granny Nothing
and the Secret Weapon

Catherine MacPhail
Illustrated by **Sarah Nayler**

■SCHOLASTIC

This one's for Baby Bob too

Scholastic Children's Books,
Commonwealth House,
1–19 New Oxford Street,
London, WC1A 1NU, UK
a division of Scholastic Ltd
London ~ New York ~ Toronto ~ Sydney ~ Auckland
Mexico City ~ New Delhi ~ Hong Kong

First published by Scholastic Ltd, 2004

Text copyright © Catherine MacPhail, 2004
Illustrations copyright © Sarah Nayler, 2004

ISBN 0 439 96336 2

All rights reserved

Typeset by M Rules
Printed and bound by AIT Nørhaven A/S, Denmark
10 9 8 7 6 5 4 3 2 1

The right of Catherine MacPhail and Sarah Nayler to be identified as the
author and illustrator of this work respectively has been asserted by
them in accordance with the Copyright, Designs and Patents Act, 1988.

This book is sold subject to the condition that it shall not,
by way of trade or otherwise, be lent, resold, hired out, or otherwise circulated
without the publisher's prior consent in any form of binding or cover other than
that in which it is published and without a similar condition, including this
condition, being imposed upon the subsequent purchaser.

Chapter One

Ewen and I were sitting with our dinner on our laps watching television. Mum was working on her computer and Dad was putting the finishing touches to his spaghetti bolognese. We had tasted Dad's cooking before, which was why we were having fish fingers in front of the telly. Dad had learned his cookery skills at his mother's knee. And since his mother was Granny Nothing, it would have taken a brave man, or a woman in love, to eat anything he cooked.

"What on earth are we watching anyway, Steph?"

Ewen asked, searching for the remote control. *"Battle of the Zombies* is on the other side."* Ewen loves zombie films. Of course, that's because he's a bit of a zombie himself.

"I want to watch this," I said. "It's educational. It's a documentary about the Berlin Wall."

"You are sad," Ewen sniffed. "You are watching a programme about a wall? Bor-ing!"

"It's not just any wall, stupid. It's a very famous wall. They pulled it down. Look!"

On the screen, the crowd were in a frenzy, hacking at the wall with hammers, with axes, breaking it up, demolishing it.

"If I did that it would be called vandalism," Ewen complained.

"It was one of the greatest moments in history," I told him. I'm always trying to improve his mind. And is he interested? No.

He just tutted. "There's not even a zombie in sight." He peered at the screen. "Although I have to say there are a lot of strange-looking people there."

A soldier with a scar thumped at the wall with his fists. A woman in an apron was hacking at it with a ladle. Granny Nothing was bashing it with a mallet. A crowd of boys were throwing stones at it. . .

Wait a minute!

"Did you see what I saw?" I asked Ewen. His mouth was hanging open.

"Did we see what we think we saw?"

Had we seen Granny Nothing on the Berlin Wall?

"It couldn't have been," I said.

"There's not many people look like Granny Nothing."

Let's face it, there's not anybody looks like Granny Nothing.

Dad came in from the kitchen just then. He was covered in bolognese sauce and had a couple of strings of spaghetti draped round his head. "Dad!" Ewen jumped to his feet. "We've just seen Granny Nothing demolishing the Berlin Wall."

Dad didn't bat an eyelid. "Of course you didn't. It wasn't my mother. Just someone who looks like her."

We reminded him that there was no one on earth who looked like Granny Nothing.

"Except maybe Stephanie," Ewen laughed. He got a good thump from me for that.

"Listen, kids, my mother is a teller of tall tales. She's never been out of the country. She doesn't even have a passport." He held out the pot. "Now, are you sure you don't want spaghetti?"

We didn't even have to think about it. "No."

Granny Nothing herself came charging in just as Dad went back into the kitchen. I say charging because she had my baby brother, Thomas on her back and he was playing at being a cowboy in a rodeo. She was a mad bull, I think.

"Granny, did we just see you on the Berlin Wall?"

Granny Nothing stopped being a bull for a moment. "Was I on that telly! I never knew they took my photo that day."

"Why were you there, Granny?"

"It's a strange and wonderful story, Ewen," she began.

Here we go again, I thought, *with the strange and wonderful stories.*

Ewen sat down again. Thomas slid to the floor. I just carried on eating my fish fingers.

"My travels had taken me to Berlin. I was there staying with Heidi, a lovely young girl, but her heart was breaking because the love of her life, Wilhelm, was stuck on the other side of that stupid wall. All she did was cry. Every day and every night. Finally, I had had enough. That wall was coming between young lovers and her greeting was driving me bonkers. So I decided then and there, it was coming down. I took a mallet from Heidi's garage and I said, 'Come on, darling, I am going to reunite you with your Wilhelm.' So off we went, and I climbed up on that wall and I just started battering lumps out of it."

"And they let you? If I'd tried that at school, Baldy would have had me arrested."

"Oh, it was dangerous, Ewen darling. The guards aimed their rifles at me. They called out to me. 'Ach-tongue! Or we shoot!' and I just shouted back. 'Ach yer tongue, yourself. Shut your gob.'"

Thomas echoed happily, "Shut your gob!"

"And then when the people saw what I was doing, it was like lighting a torch of freedom. Out came the hammers and the shovels, and the offensive weapons. Before you could say Granny Nothing, that wall was covered with folk bringing it down."

"And were Heidi and Wilhelm reunited?" Ewen asked.

"Unfortunately not. Heidi took one look at him and he'd put on so much weight she did a runner back to West Berlin."

"I love a happy ending," I said.

"So why didn't you get the credit, Granny Nothing, for bringing down the Berlin Wall? And what were you doing in Berlin in the first place?"

She did a strange thing then. I know, everything she does is strange, but this took me by surprise. She didn't tell us a weird and wonderful story for once. Instead, she put one of her big chip fingers to her lips, and her eyes darted from left to right as if someone might be listening. "Ssssh," she said. "That's a secret never to be told."

And she charged out of the room again with Thomas roaring on her back.

Ewen just stared at me. "Why didn't she have a story about that one?" he asked.

"I don't know," I said, because that bothered me too. "There are too many secrets with Granny Nothing, and I think it's about time we found out the truth."

"How?" Ewen asked. He could never figure anything out for himself.

"Something Dad said has got me thinking. We've never seen her passport, have we? Well, I intend to find it."

"How are you going to do that, Steph?"

"We're going to look in Granny Nothing's suitcase."

Ewen didn't look too happy about that. "Oh no, Steph, every time we open that case something weird happens."

That strange case she had brought with her the night she arrived out of nowhere, and scared the living daylights out of everyone. It had labels plastered all over it from remote and exotic places, and some places that weren't so exotic, or even remote. (Although when you think of it, nowhere is remote if you live in it, is it?) Inside the case were all sorts of weird and wonderful objects. A shrunken head, a rusty key, a Sioux head-dress, but never had I seen any sign of a passport.

"We should have looked for it before. I don't know why I didn't think of it."

Ewen put his arm around my shoulders. "Don't worry, Steph. You can't help it if you're not the sharpest tool in the box."

"What!" I gave him a punch that sent him flying off the sofa, and his fish fingers with him. "You're the one that's thick in this family."

Suddenly there was the most horrendous noise from the other room and we both ran in to see what it was.

Granny Nothing was standing clasping her hands together, almost in tears. "Listen to my boy! He's making music. I think he's going to be a child prodigy." (She pronounced it "proditchy".)

The child "proditchy" was battering lumps out of a toy xylophone with his toy guitar. The noise he was making brought tears to my eyes.

"A child prodigy?" I said. "He can't walk. The only

words he can say are 'Grrrranny', and 'Hells Bells and Buckets', and 'wurrums'. Oh yes, and 'shut your gob'. Let's face it, the boy's an idiot," I told her.

Granny Nothing waved that away. "The boy can't be good at everything, Steph."

By this time, Thomas was dribbling and trying to put the guitar in his mouth, sideways. Granny Nothing gazed at him fondly. "That's my boy," she said.

Chapter Two

You took your life in your hands crossing the street to our school every day. Cars used it as a shortcut to the motorway. They raced along it as if they were in the Grand Prix, and nothing, not speed bumps, or flashing lights, or even sleeping policeman slowed them down.

So they certainly never took any notice of Mrs Bradley, our lollipop lady.

She would gather us all together on the pavement, her face almost the same colour as her yellow coat. Fear does that to you.

She would cock her ears, listening for cars. Then, she would lift her lollipop high like a flag of truce. "Right, children, now. Make a run for it."

And we would. Dashing across the street as if our lives depended on it. And of course, they did. Usually, there would be a roar from round the corner when we were halfway across. Mrs Bradley would wave her lollipop around madly. "Back, children. Back!" And though we were halfway across we would dart back to the other side.

Just in time or there might have been a massacre.

Same this morning. We had only made it back on to the pavement when a sleek black convertible whizzed past us.

"Don't you know this is a lollipop!" Mrs Bradley yelled after him.

The driver made a very rude gesture out of his window.

But let's face it. A lollipop is hardly an offensive weapon, is it? You're hardly likely to strike fear into the heart of a passing motorist with a lollipop, are you?

Now, if they gave Mrs Bradley a ray-gun, or a machete, that might be a different matter.

She tried again. "Come along, children. Chop-chop."

We all chop-chopped into the middle of the road again.

There was a screech and a squealing of tyres and a bright red sports car did a wheelie round the corner.

"Ah!" Mrs Bradley screamed. "Back! Back!"

We all raced back, pulling Mrs Bradley with us. Just

in time too. Or she would have ended up a yellow stripe in the road.

"I can't take much more of this," she wailed, leaning against the wall, sweat pouring from her. "Something has to be done about the traffic in this street."

"Is it always this interesting getting in to your school?" Elvis asked. He'd been transferred to our school because it was nearer home. This was his first day. And already he thought it was a wonderful adventure.

"No," I said, "sometimes it's *really* exciting."

We finally made it across the street, almost carrying Mrs Bradley with us. We left her in the first-aid room having a cup of tea.

Baldy, our headmaster, gathered us all together for morning assembly. All he could talk about was the upcoming rugby match, the first leg of the final, between our school team, the Mini Maulers, and our rivals, the Burrington Bears.

"I'm not worried. We have a wonderful team. We're bound to win the inter-schools' trophy."

The man was an idiot. Our team was rubbish. Ewen was considered our star player, and you could blow him over in a light breeze. The only reason we had even made it to this final was because we had never actually played a match! The first team we were supposed to play started a fight between themselves and they were disqualified. The second team put two professionals on in the hope no one would notice. I think the beards gave them away, personally. Anyway, they were disqualified too. The next team decided at the last minute they thought rugby was a daft game, and pulled out to play in the football tournament. A very wise decision, in my opinion.

So, here we were, the Mini Maulers, ready to take on the mighty Burrington Bears, and we had never kicked a rugby ball over the bar once.

Baldy was now welcoming Elvis into our school.

"And I want you all to make the new boy, Elvis Singh, feel at home. Be nice to him. Show him what lovely people we are in this school."

"I should be in the team," Elvis said, hardly listening. "I'm good at rugby."

One thing about the Singh family, our Elvis Presley lookalike neighbours (although between you and me they look no more like him than Granny Nothing looks like Marilyn Monroe), they thought they were good at everything.

Ewen said smugly, "You would have to pass a really hard test to get in."

"Have you got two feet, Elvis?" I asked him. "Yes? OK, you've passed the test."

Everyone laughed except Ewen, and maybe Polly and Todd Dangerfield. Let's face it, only Elvis and I laughed.

Elvis looked Ewen up and down. "Well, if you got in the team they must be desperate. You're a wimp."

"What did you call him?" It was Polly, standing in front of us, and she had heard it all.

"I said, he's a wimp."

Polly stood with her hands on her hips, glaring at Elvis.

Baldy had started to sing one of the school songs, the one about what a lovely morning it was and how wonderful school was too. No one joined in.

All at once a painful howl joined in with Baldy's painful howl of a song. The howl of a soul in torment.

"What on earth is that?" I asked.

We all looked into the street outside. There was Presley, his paws on a lamp post, and he was howling in anguish.

"He's missing me," Elvis said.

"Whose dog is that?" Baldy shouted. His eyes went straight to Elvis. "Is no one looking after your dog while you're at school?"

"Yes," Elvis said. "Nanny. . ."

He didn't get her name out. Suddenly Nanny Sue appeared on the scene, and she looked annoyed as she clipped Presley's lead on to his collar. She tried to drag him away. Presley didn't want to go. His big brown eyes were focused into the assembly hall, on Elvis. Elvis's big brown eyes were focused out on the street, on Presley.

"He knows it's my first day here. He's worried about me." Elvis waved, and that set Presley off. He began to bound along the street trying to get a better view of Elvis. Personally, I thought he was just showing off. Nanny Sue was caught off guard. She was suddenly dragged screaming after him.

"What did you call Ewen?" Polly pulled at Elvis.

Elvis had almost forgotten her. "I called him a wimp," Elvis said calmly, still waving at Presley.

"Right, that's it!" Polly suddenly jumped on Elvis, taking him completely by surprise. She started battering him with her schoolbag. Presley saw what was happening and tried to leap over the school gates to get in to help Elvis. He dragged Nanny Sue behind him. She was caught on the gates, screaming for help. The assembly hall went wild. Baldy tried to calm everyone down. Didn't work.

Polly was all over Elvis like a rash, like a sudden attack of chickenpox.

"Put that boy down, Polly! I told you to make him feel welcome!" Baldy shouted.

Polly and Elvis were locked in mortal combat. Presley was careering back and forth past the window dragging a screaming Nanny Sue behind him. I could see Mrs Bradley being carried out of the school on a stretcher.

Total chaos.

Pandemonium.

But just another ordinary day in the life of the McAllisters.

Chapter Three

"We're never going to win that match," Ewen said as we walked home. "It's useless."

Elvis looked around to make sure Polly wasn't within earshot before he agreed. "Completely hopeless."

Elvis already had been drafted on to the team, even without a tryout. It didn't matter how bad he was, he had to be better than what we had.

Presley was bounding all around him, happy at last. Nanny Sue fumed her way home behind us. She still hadn't recovered. Her hair was standing on end and she had broken the heel of her shoe. She had been dragged back and forth along the street all day. "Hate that dog!" she kept saying breathlessly. "He could have killed me."

I told her to look on the bright side. "Pop stars would pay a fortune for a workout like that."

There had to be something we could do to help our team. When we went home, Ewen and I decided to ask Granny Nothing. She always had a solution.

"She"ll probably tell us she used to be a rugby player. She's certainly built like one. No neck and a voice like a volcano ready to erupt."

We were wrong. She had never been a rugby player, and even more amazing, no rugby player had ever fallen madly in love with her. "Och no, darlings," she had said when we asked her. "I'm too much of a lady to play rugby. I'm just a gentle soul at heart."

This, from the woman who claimed to have been a champion sumo wrestler, and to have tackled rampaging alligators in the Florida Everglades.

Today, she was dressed in a bright orange trouser suit. Thomas was sitting on her head like a hat, or perhaps an orange cowpat, and judging by the smell that was more appropriate.

"What your team needs is a coach," she told us.

Ewen looked baffled. "What do we need a bus for?"

The boy is thick. "A coach, to train us . . . a training coach."

Now, we already had a coach, and Granny Nothing

15

knew it. Baldy, he was our coach. No wonder we were rubbish.

"No, I mean a real coach. A real Maori coach. Boy, can they play rugby."

"Unfortunately, not a lot of Maoris live around here," I reminded her.

"I'll find one for you." She tapped her nose. "I've got contacts. Meanwhile," she went on. "I am going to organize the cheerleaders."

I gasped. "The cheerleaders? Don't tell me you plan to be a cheerleader?"

"I think my pompoms are still in my case," she said, dreamily.

Her case. I glanced at my brother. It had reminded us of our plan. We were going to look in that case for her passport.

Before tea, when we were supposed to be doing our homework, I dragged Ewen out to the garage. Granny Nothing's case had been moved once again. From the cupboard at the top of the stairs to the cellar, and now it was in our garage piled between other cases and boxes.

As we sneaked inside Nanny Sue caught sight of us. "What are you two looking so suspicious about?" She was peering at us over the Singhs' hedge and she looked pretty suspicious herself. She was probably trying to hide from Presley.

"We're in our own garden," I told her. "We can look suspicious if we want."

Her beady eyes followed us all the way.

"I don't trust her," Ewen said. "She wants to find out Granny Nothing's secret too."

And that was the truth. Granny Nothing *had* a secret. Where had she been all those years when we had never even known she existed? Where had she gone? What had she done? According to Dad she had only been living in a wee flat in Glasgow, and going to her bingo on a Saturday night. But that didn't sound like the Granny Nothing we knew.

Even among an assortment of other cases Granny Nothing's was easy to spot. Labels were plastered all over it. Honolulu, Dubrovnik, Barlinnie. Faraway places with strange sounding names.

I stood on a box and pulled it down from the shelf. I laid it on the floor of the garage and snapped it open.

It never failed to amaze me the things she kept in that case: a grass skirt, a boomerang, a voodoo mask. Every time we looked, it seemed we found something new and it always led to another adventure. The Shrunken Head. The Rusty Key. This time there was a walking stick I had never seen before, ornate carved wood with a silver handle.

Ewen lifted it to look more closely. "It's a very short walking stick," he said. "It must be for a pygmy." He turned it around, and seemed to touch some kind of switch on the handle. Suddenly the tip came off to reveal a long steel stiletto blade.

"Wow!" Ewen almost fell back. "That's dangerous. How did she get a thing like that?"

I quickly put the top back on and slipped it into the case again. For the moment, I didn't want to know where she got that. But I might, someday.

As always she had an assortment of silk knickers, blue and red (her favourite colour) and pink and green. Frilled and embroidered and laced. Boy, she loved her knickers.

I pushed them aside gingerly. Ewen refused to touch them at all.

"Well, there's no pompoms here," Ewen said, when we had searched through the whole case.

"And no passport." I wasn't the least bit surprised. I had known she wouldn't have a passport. All her stories were lies. I had never believed them anyway.

So, why was I so disappointed?

"You didn't look in there." Ewen pointed to a zipped-up pocket at the back of her case. "Maybe we'll find some love letters from all those men who've fallen madly in love with her."

At that moment, I didn't care what we found. It would all be part of the lie. Granny Nothing was just your typical terrifying rhinoceros of a granny who told tall tales. Nothing weird or wonderful had ever really happened to her.

I unzipped the pocket and reached inside.

And I gasped.

And Ewen gasped.

Because we had found, at last, Granny Nothing's passport.

And not just one.
And not just two.
Granny Nothing had seven passports.

Chapter Four

Ewen fell back on the floor. "Seven passports, Stephanie! Why has she got seven passports?"

I was trying to understand it myself. Were they real? I looked at them more closely, one by one. Expecting to see "Citizen of Toytown" printed on the front.

But no, one was a British passport. One was a United States passport. One was Spanish. One was printed in the funniest-looking alphabet I had ever seen. I think it was Russian. I was just about to open it and see what name, what photograph was inside when a voice shrieked out. "What have you got there!"

It was Nanny Sue. She had followed us into the garage and she took me so much by surprise that I dropped the passports. Immediately, I sat on them. They would be just what Nanny Sue would want to add to her "portfolio" against Granny Nothing.

The best form of defence is attack, so I snapped at Nanny Sue, "What are you doing in here? You're trespassing."

She didn't even answer me. She pushed me aside and dropped to her knees. Her eyes flashed when she saw the open suitcase. She didn't seem interested in the passports and I realized that she hadn't even seen them. "It's her case," she said. "The one she brought with her that first night she arrived. I've always wondered what was inside."

Ewen tried to snap the case shut. Nanny Sue's fingers got in the way. She let out a yelp and gave Ewen a shove. "You did that on purpose." She flung the lid open once again. "Now, what's in here," she said. She pushed aside the Sioux headdress, Granny Nothing's assortment of multicoloured knickers, and a broken mirror. Her face crumpled in disappointment. "Junk," she said. "It's a caseload of old junk."

Ewen took it personally. "It is not junk! It's. . ."

I zipped my lips to make him keep quiet. Let Nanny Sue think what she liked.

"What did you expect?" I asked her. "Gold? Silver? A dismembered body perhaps?"

"I expected something more interesting than this."

She picked up the voodoo mask and put it on her face. Her eyes inside it looked weird. She flashed them at us. "I'll put a spell on you!" she said in a crazy voice.

I half expected that the mask would cling to her face, that it would be stuck there for ever, or that when she did take it off, her own face would have changed into something horrible – or even more horrible in Nanny Sue's case.

But when she flung the mask back into the case she was still the same old ugly Nanny Sue.

She took the Sioux headdress next. "She must have bought this for Halloween. In some old second-hand shop."

She lifted the broken mirror. "Ha! I wouldn't think she'd ever want to look at that ugly face of hers."

She dropped the mirror back into the case. "What's this?" And she picked out something else I had never seen in the case before. A miniature mummy, like a little doll, all wrapped up in bandages. "It's the mummy's curse!" she yelled and she rolled her eyes as if she was quite mad, which of course she is.

All at once she let out a cry of pain. "Oh, there's a pin in that thing! Look, it's made me bleed." She held up her finger.

"Maybe it bit you," Ewen said hopefully.

She threw the mummy doll back into the case. "It's only junk!" she said again. "But at least I know there's nothing interesting in here at all."

She was sucking at her finger where a spot of blood had appeared. "You should throw that case out," she said. "It's probably full of germs."

As she got to her feet, a roar like thunder rent the air. "What's that?"

"It's Granny Nothing calling us in for our tea."

Nanny Sue began to panic then. She pushed us in front of her for protection.

The passports lay on the floor. I kicked them under the case to hide them from view. We left along with Nanny Sue, there was no other choice. We would have to come back for the passports later.

Granny Nothing was at the kitchen door calling for us. Nanny Sue leaped over the hedge into the comparative safety of next door's garden. Safe, but not for long. We heard Presley barking excitedly, and Nanny Sue screaming for help.

Granny Nothing was now all in red. Her dress was red, her wrinkly stockings were red, she even wore a red bandanna . . . no, wait a minute, that was Thomas, wrapped round her head, all in red too. I think she was trying to look like an Italian peasant. It wasn't working. She only looked like a rhinoceros dressed up to look like an Italian peasant.

"Corri! Corri!" she shouted when she spotted us. "Tonight, we eat Italian!"

And before we could stop her, she started singing.

I hunted in my pockets for a spare pair of earplugs, but just my luck, I had forgotten them.

"Macaroni, pepperoni,
Vermicelli in my belly
Eata pizza margharita
Every notte for my tea.

Hot panini tortellini
I'ma crazy for Bolognese
In my glory with cacciatore
Every notte for my tea.

I lova Italian
I lova Italian
I lova Italian
For my tea!!!!!"

All the time she was singing she was dancing around the kitchen banging a spoon on to a plate. Ewen, caught up with the music (music, ha!), grabbed a pot and began dancing after her.

What was the point of being the only sensible one in the family? I grabbed a pot and followed them.

"Cannelloni, rigatoni
Calamari, carbonara
I get blotto on my risotto
Every notte for my tea!

I lova Italian
I lova Italian
I lova Italian

Forra mya. . ."

"Big finish!" she yelled.

"TEA!!!!!!!!!"

Thomas was screaming and dribbling with excitement. She lifted him from her head. "Listen to that boy. Do you hear that voice. He's got perfect pitch. He's a miniature Paravotti! He's a child proditchy, I tell ye."

At that point Thomas was sitting on the floor trying to figure out which end of the spoon to put in his mouth.

"It's Pavarotti, actually," I said, my voice full of sarcasm.

Lost on Granny Nothing as usual.

"Aye, you can see it as well, Steph, darlin'." She looked at Thomas lovingly. "The boy's a genius."

After tea, Ewen pulled me into the conservatory. "When are you going to ask her about the passports?"

"What's the point?" I asked him. "She'll only lie. She'll have some fantastic story to tell us. Anyway, we're not even sure if they're her passports. We didn't get a chance to look with that stupid Nanny Sue disturbing us."

Ewen peeked into the kitchen. Granny Nothing was still there, trying to teach the child prodigy how to lick his plate clean. "We could sneak into the garage now, and have a good look."

So we did.

We tiptoed inside, and we searched everywhere. In every corner of the garage, on every shelf, in every box.

But we found nothing.

The passports had gone, and so had Granny Nothing's case.

Chapter Five

The morning of the match dawned bright and clear. Granny Nothing made her appearance with a wild, "TARA!" Now, I have seen Granny Nothing in some weird and wonderful outfits. I have even seen her in a thong and let me tell you that is not a sight for the fainthearted. But I have never seen Granny Nothing in anything so daft as her cheerleader outfit. She looked like a bright yellow pompom all by herself. She was wearing a short pleated skirt. "It shows off my legs," she said. "I've seen men faint at the sight of my legs." That didn't surprise me. They looked like monster tree trunks come to life. She was wearing a fluffy yellow sweater that was making everybody sneeze. And she was waving her pompoms about wildly.

"Where did you get those?" I asked her.

"In my case," she said at once. "You remember my case?"

Was she trying to tell us something? Did she know that we had been in her case, found her passports? Was she the one who had moved it?

Now was the moment to confront her about those passports, solve the mystery. Although I was still convinced she'd probably had them printed at "fakepassports.com". But there was something apart from her outfit that put all thought of passports out of my head.

Her hair.

It was standing out in gelled spikes all over her head. She looked like a demented version of the Statue of Liberty.

"Is that not just lovely?" she asked.

"I've never seen anything like it," Ewen mumbled.

Granny Nothing grinned. "I'm trying to look funky. I want to change my image. I want to be bold, adventurous, daring!"

With that she leaped about the kitchen waving her pompoms about dangerously. For the first time I noticed Thomas. He was strapped to her back, in yellow T-shirt and dungarees which blended in beautifully with her outfit. She had spiked his hair to match hers. She'd even supplied him with a couple of mini pompoms.

"I never want to embarrass you by being ordinary," she said.

No fear of that, ever.

"Right," she yelled. "Come on, Ewen, you are going to be man of the match!"

Ewen shook his head. "We're going to get slaughtered, Granny."

"Come on, son." She squeezed his shoulder. "Think positive. That's why you need a cheerleader. I'm going to fire you up to win."

And she did her best to do just that. But the other team, The Burrington Bears, were built like . . . well, like bears actually. Even with Elvis drafted on to the team, our best player (mind you, we had discovered he was rubbish as well), we didn't stand a chance.

Granny Nothing threw her pompoms around like hand grenades. She bounced up and down and almost caused an earthquake. We had prayed that once again Fate would intervene and something terrible might happen to the other team and the match would have to be abandoned. But to our complete shock, we were actually expected to play.

You could see our team were trying to remember exactly what they were supposed to do. What were the rules of the game? What was a try? What was a scrum?

Useless! Every last one of them.

When the match began was when the real trouble started. Granny Nothing kept running on to the field whenever anyone tackled Ewen. "Leave my boy be!" she would shout, lifting players from him by the scruff of the neck.

The other team's coach, Coach Muldoon, was fuming. He bawled at her every time. "Get that woman . . . or whatever it is, off this field!"

Dad kept having to yank her away. "She did the same thing for me when I was in the football team. Wouldn't let anybody near me. It was really embarrassing."

"But he's only wee," Granny Nothing wailed, watching Ewen. "He's the wee-est boy on the field. He could get hurted," she said.

"He could get hurt," I corrected her.

She patted my shoulder. "I know, you're worried about him as well."

Needless to say, we were slaughtered. The score was . . . mmmm. . .

I don't understand rugby scores. Actually I think it's a stupid game. I much prefer football. Anyway, whatever the score was, we lost.

Even with Granny Nothing's demented cheerleading, and Mrs Singh's banners and their singing at half time (mind you, personally I think that really put our team off), we couldn't score a try, or even try to score. We were slaughtered.

Our supporters, all twenty of them, sat with glum faces, while the other team's supporters stamped and roared. "They don't have to be so pleased with themselves," I said. I hate bad winners.

However, Granny Nothing insisted that we all go and congratulate the other team. "That's playing the game!" she said. We waited till they filed out of their dressing room led by Coach Muldoon. He had a tuft of white hair and a set of white teeth to match. One of them wasn't real, the hair or the teeth, I don't know which.

Granny Nothing put out her hand to congratulate him. He pushed her away. "Here, boys, I bet you didn't know the other team had a hippopotamus as their mascot!" He roared with laughter and, following suit, so did his team.

Granny Nothing growled.

"I bet when she was born the doctor slapped her face mistaking it for her backside! How much do you bet, boys?"

The team roared with laughter again.

They were now so bold as to try their own insults. "Look at that hair."

Suddenly something flew through the air towards Granny Nothing. I screamed, sure it was a stone. It wasn't. It was a doughnut. It landed perfectly on one of her spikes. There was a scream of laughter from the other team.

"Go on, boys," Coach Muldoon egged them on. "I bet you can't get a doughnut on each of her spikes."

One, two, three more doughnuts flew through the air. They all landed perfectly. Granny Nothing began to seethe. "I'm getting angry now, and you won't like me when I'm angry."

Baldy stepped forward. "I don't think this is suitable behaviour for a coach," he said to Coach Muldoon.

Coach Muldoon lifted him from the ground. "How much do you bet, boys? Does he weigh as much as an empty paper bag?"

Granny Nothing had had enough. I could see she was ready to explode. "I bet that if you and your team aren't in that bus in ten seconds your body parts will be flying round this place."

Now they were afraid, very afraid. They began to run towards the bus. Granny Nothing was after them, her doughnuts bouncing on her spikes. Only the door of the bus snapping shut saved them. I could see she was ready to lift the bus, tip it over. I stopped her just in time. "They're not worth it, Granny," I told her.

So instead, she thumped the side of the bus and put a dent in it. "I'll be seeing you in the second leg and I'll make you very sorry you made fun of a poor old woman and her beautiful hair."

Then her roar seemed to come from deep within her. "Granny Nothing'll get you for this!"

The bus screeched off with the other team still making faces at us while Coach Muldoon bet them who could come up with the worst insult.

Ewen took her hand. "I don't think you're ugly, Granny. I think you're the best granny in the world."

I was expecting maybe a tear in her eye when she

turned to us. Being called a hippopotamus might do that to a person.

Granny Nothing feeling sorry for herself? You must be joking.

"Of course I'm not ugly, son. I'm bootiful." She said. Then she took a doughnut from one of her spikes and bit into it. "Delicious. Anybody else want one?"

Chapter Six

We were all late for school next day. Mrs Bradley, the lollipop lady, was on sick leave. Stress, we were told. So, there was no one to help us to cross the street.

A couple of brave parents turned up and even managed to get a few of the little ones across in one mad dash.

Baldy wailed, "We have got to do something about the traffic on this street!"

When we went home Granny Nothing had the perfect solution.

"I'll be your lollipop lady," she said.

I was waiting for one of her "this reminds me of the time I was lollipopping in Outer Mongolia" kind of stories. But no. She actually admitted she had never been a lollipop lady.

"But I've stopped traffic before. When you've got a face and figure like mine you're bound to. You'll be the same, Stephanie. You're turning into a carbon copy of your Granny."

No! I'd dye my hair. Have my teeth fixed. Anything but that.

I wonder how much plastic surgery would cost?

However, there was something taking her interest even more than the school traffic.

"I've found the perfect man." She had, it seemed, been locked along with Thomas in her room all day. Every so often Mum had heard her roar and laugh. Now as we sat having tea she came bounding out, her hair still in spikes, one solitary doughnut still lodged there.

"You've found what?"

"The perfect man!" she repeated. "I've been on the wurruldwide web looking for one, and I've found him."

First, I have to say I was surprised she'd been looking for a man at all. Second, what kind of shock would she be to any man she found? But third and most important, we were always being warned about meeting people through the internet.

"Granny," I said. "If you want a man, I'm sure you could get one at a reputable dating agency."

She threw her head back and laughed. (What a daft expression. Of course she didn't actually take her head in both hands and chuck it over her shoulder!)

"Godluvye! Not that kind of man. I've had one of them. Your daddy's faither. He was useless." And again I was reminded that there once had been a man brave enough to marry Granny Nothing.

"I've been online," she said. "At rugbycoaches.com. And here he is." She produced a page she had printed off. It was a photograph of the biggest, meanest-looking Maori I had ever seen. He was almost as scary-looking as Granny Nothing herself.

"He's called Maurice the Mauler." She said.

"Maurice? What a name for a mauler," I said, disappointed.

"I think it's an omen that his nickname is the Mauler. He's going to coach the Mini Maulers. He's coming over next week to meet up with his email girlfriend. She's called Estelle. She's a make-up artiste —" she pronounced it art-eest — "in a horror film studio. And he's agreed to coach our team for the next match."

"He looks a bit fierce." Ewen said, then he looked up at Granny Nothing and grinned. "But you look a lot fiercer."

"Sorted!" Granny Nothing said. "We'll win that trophy by hook or by rook."

"You mean by crook or by book," Ewen said.

"You're both wrong. It's by rook or by. . . Oh bother, I can't remember myself now."

"I'll come to the school tomorrow and be your

lollipop lady, and I'll tell Baldy all about him. But," and at this she put her finger to her lips and whispered, "no one must know what he's really here for. Because Maurice is going to be our Secret Weapon!"

Secrets! As soon as she said it I remembered the passports. I decided there was no time, like right at this very present, as she would say, to confront her.

"We were in your case, Granny, and we saw the passports," I said. "All seven of them."

"Were they real? Were they yours? How come you've got seven?" Ewen asked breathlessly.

"Och . . . it's a secret son. I cannot really say a word. You see, I've signed the Fishul Secrets Act."

Ewen looked baffled. "Fishul secrets? What's that?"

"She means . . . the Official Secrets Act," I told him. I'm always having to translate for her. "And what would you be doing signing the Official Secrets Act?"

I braced myself for another strange and wonderful story. It wasn't long in coming. Ewen sat down, and I lay along the floor. *Might as well be comfortable,* I thought.

"It all began when I had a wee part-time job in a central African state. I was the canteen lady in a factory there. Oh, they loved my cooking in that canteen." Obviously a central African state for the brain dead if they enjoyed her cooking. "They would come running in and shouting, 'I'll have roast wildebeest and Yorkshire pudding, Granny.' Or, 'I'll have your python salad and chips.' And I would roar back at them. 'Get in that line or you'll get nothing from Granny Nothing.'"

She sighed at the memory. "Och," she went on, "they were a nice bunch of boys. Except for one. Magoomba was his name. He was a bad lot. I had to chuck him out every day. 'You'll be sorry for this!' he would shout. I never trusted him. I decided to keep my eye on him, because Magoomba was up to something. I could tell. Well, one day, El Presidente himself visited my canteen. Oh, it was a great honour. We blew up balloons for him, and we hung up banners. Cooked him a special meal and everything. Mashed maggots and fricassee of daddy-long-legs, if I remember right. Everybody was looking forward to him coming. The big day finally arrived, and in he strode, oh such a nice wee man, waving his wee feather duster around the place and smiling."

"His 'wee feather duster'?" Ewen asked. "What was he, a part-time cleaner?"

This sent Granny Nothing laughing so loudly I thought she was going to wet herself. "Not at all. Only high-class people carry them things. I think they keep the flies off them. "

I nudged my brother. "Let her get on with the story."

She didn't need telling twice. "Suddenly, out of the blue . . . well, out of my onion cupboard actually, leaped Magoomba screaming and yelling and waving a machete about like a lethal weapon."

(Isn't a machete a lethal weapon anyway, I wondered?)

"He was going to assissin . . . assesserate . . . assign . . . he was going to kill El Presidente!" she said it dramatically. Thomas was dribbling all over her with excitement. Ewen's mouth was hanging open. Am I the only one who isn't taken in by her stories?

"What happened next, Granny?" Ewen asked her.

"I'll tell ye what happened. I leaped into action. . ."

With that she jumped in the air and the last doughnut dislodged itself from her spike and flew across the room. "I grabbed his machete and I broke it in two. I wasn't having any bloodshed in my canteen. It would have made a right mess of my vulture vol au vents."

(She pronounced them volley vongs.)

"So I grabbed Magoomba, I swung him round my head, and I locked him back in the cupboard. Well, El Presidente was that grateful he offered to make me his bride. But I had to turn him down . . . he already had twenty-three wives. 'I am a one-woman man, El Presidente,' I tells him. But somebody from MI5 was there, Sir Samuel Simmons of the Secret Service, and he was that impressed with me, he asked me to come and work for MI5 . . . undercover, so to speak. And that was the beginning of my career with the secret service."

"So you're kind of like James Bond?" Ewen sounded excited.

"Exactly son. I am the Granny Nothing version of James Bond. But no one must ever know."

Except, of course, me and Ewen and Thomas.

"Does that mean we have to sign the Fishul Secrets Act now too?" I asked her.

"Oh no, Stephanie darling. I mean if I can't trust my grandchildren, who can I trust?"

Granny Nothing stood up and looked off into the sunset. She stood proud and tall. "Whenever they need somebody to sneak into a country, to do a bit of rescuing and that, I am given the call. I could disappear at a minute's notice." She snapped her fingers. "Just like that. I would have to drop everything, and go. I am what you might call . . . the other Secret Weapon."

Chapter Seven

The very next day was Granny's first as our lollipop lady. She was in the full rig-out. The yellow coat, the peaked cap, the lollipop. She looked very impressive.

So did Thomas. He had on a mini version of the uniform, lollipop and all.

As we began to cross the road she held us back.

"You can't cross now," she said. "There's no motors coming." Thomas sat on her shoulders and held his yellow lollipop in the air. It had bits of Granny Nothing's hair attached to it, but that only seemed to make it more enjoyable for Thomas. Honestly, he is disgusting!

"I've got a plan!" Granny Nothing told us. "Just do everything I tell you, and your traffic troubles will be terminated."

Well, she'd never let us down before. Why shouldn't we trust her now?

So, we waited.

Five minutes later, and rush hour began in earnest.

One, two, three cars whooshed round the corner. Granny Nothing went into action like a speeding bullet. She spread herself across the road like an enormous yellow toad, holding her lollipop as if it was a lethal weapon. "Stopppppp!" she roared. The first car screeched to a halt. Then the second. Then the third. They almost crashed into each other.

Granny Nothing smiled sweetly at the drivers. "Thank you, gentlemen."

Then she ushered us across the road, very slowly. "Take your time children. Slowly now. Don't want any of you wee ones to fall and hurt yourself."

The first driver leaned out of his window. "Get out of my way! I'm in a hurry."

The second driver echoed that. "So am I."

"Me too!" shouted the third. Granny Nothing ignored them until each of us was safely on the other side. Then she turned to the waiting cars, who were revving up their engines angrily. There were at least ten of them now. All hooting their horns and shouting abuse.

"If you were in such a hurry, you should have tooken another road."

"They should have taken another road," I corrected her.

"See, my wee granddaughter agrees with me."

"But this is a shortcut!" the first driver yelled.

Granny Nothing suddenly looked wicked. She looked the way she had on that first stormy night when she'd arrived at our house. She looked scary. She certainly scared those drivers. A couple of them slid their windows up . . . just in case.

"Not now it isn't," she said.

Still, she wouldn't let the cars pass. "Oh, hold on, here come a couple of stragglers."

I'm sure some of the cars might have risked sneaking round her. But if her body came into contact with their cars, the cars would come off worse. It wasn't worth the risk.

She did the exact same thing when we came out of school. She caused a major traffic jam as cars lined up the street, the queue going back right on to the motorway. It made no difference to Granny Nothing. She insisted we all take our time and crossed the road slowly, admiring the view.

"We'll go to the council about this!" the drivers complained.

"Go!" she shouted back. "But don't take this road if you want to get there on time."

Then she heehawed with laughter so loudly we all joined her.

It had turned out a most successful day. She had protected her children, terrified quite a few people, and now Granny Nothing was looking forward to Maurice's arrival. "Oh, if we get a Maori to be our coach we're bound to win, Ewen," she said, then she slapped him on the back and he fell off the couch.

I decided then that if Maurice the Maori Mauler helped our team of wimps to win that trophy I would rename him Maurice the Miracle Man.

Chapter Eight

Maurice arrived three days later. He was coming in on the five o'clock train and Granny Nothing took me and Ewen and Thomas (naturally, when does she ever go anywhere without Thomas, the Siamese grandson?) to the station to meet him. Mum was preparing a special Maori meal to welcome him, though between you and me she hadn't a clue what a special Maori meal was, and Dad was having a snooze in the front room.

We were travelling undercover. Granny Nothing said that since Maurice was our Secret Weapon no one must know that he was here. We were sworn to secrecy. Even Thomas was sworn to secrecy, though I don't know why she was worried about him. No one ever understood a word he said.

Undercover. That meant that Granny Nothing was wearing her special secret service raincoat. She also wore a hat pulled down over her face, and a pair of sunglasses.

"I don't want anybody to recognize me," she said.

It didn't work. The whole way she kept bumping into people. That was the sunglasses. She couldn't see a thing through them.

"Sorry, Granny Nothing, my fault entirely," everyone said.

Or, "You suit your hat, Granny Nothing."

Or, "Thomas has just fallen off, Granny Nothing."

Thomas couldn't see anything either. He was wearing sunglasses too.

Granny Nothing showed us the photo of Maurice again. "You'll never miss him," she said.

She was right about that. Maurice closely resembled a monster gorilla with toothache.

The five o'clock train pulled into the station and we scanned every face as the people came off the train. I could see no one who resembled a monster gorilla with or without toothache.

Two little old ladies got off, arguing about who was going to carry the shopping bags. They ended up trying to pull them off each other in the middle of the platform.

"Let me have them, Mavis."

"No, Louise, I'll take them, I insist."

A vicar stepped on to the platform and fell flat on his face.

And there was a tiny wee man, struggling to lift his case out of the carriage.

But no gorilla.

"Maybe he's missed his train," I suggested.

"Maybe he's in disguise as well," Ewen said.

The two old ladies were now on the ground, battling it out with each other.

"I'll carry them, Mavis!"

"Over my dead body, Louise!"

The vicar was running towards them. "Ladies, please."

Granny Nothing was watching the little man struggling with his case.

"Och here, I'm away to help that poor wee soul."

He just couldn't get that case out of the carriage at all. And the train was almost ready to move off. One more minute and that case of his would be travelling on to the next station without him.

Granny Nothing lifted his case with one hand and heaved it on to the platform.

He couldn't have been more grateful. "Oh, I can't thank you enough. I thought for a minute that my bag was going to go off with the train."

Right at that moment the train started to move, and so did he. His coat was caught in the doors. He ran in reverse, faster and faster as the train gathered speed. His little legs going like the clappers. (What are the clappers, I wonder?)

His eyes began to pop. He screeched, "Help!"

Granny Nothing was after him in a flash. It never ceases to amaze me how fast she can move for a woman the size of Moby Dick. There was nothing going to stop that train, so she grabbed the man, and began unbuttoning his coat. With one yank she pulled him out of it.

"That's my good new coat," the little man said.

"Ach, d'ye want to run backwards all the way to the next station?"

We stood watching as his coat flapped its way into a tunnel. It was almost as if it was waving goodbye. Granny Nothing patted him on the back and almost sent him flying on to the track. "See me, son," she said, grabbing him by the collar as he began to sway dangerously. "I just have a knack of sorting out people's problems."

I looked up and down the platform for Maurice. By this time the two old ladies had turned on the vicar who'd tried to separate them. They were both battering him with their handbags.

"You leave my friend Mavis alone!"

"I'll teach you to speak like that to my friend Louise!"

Apart from that the platform was deserted.

"Maybe he missed his train," Ewen suggested.

"Maybe he decided not to come," I said.

Granny Nothing shook her head. Thomas wobbled on her shoulders. "Naw, a Maori's word is sacred. If Maurice said he'd come, he'll come."

The little man who was still trying to lift his case tugged at her sleeve. "Did you say Maurice?"

"Aye, a big fierce-looking Maori? Was on he on that train?"

At this point he looked kind of scared. "Actually, I'm Maurice."

Sniff

Chapter Nine

This then was our secret weapon. He looked like an anorexic stick insect. He was also wearing beer-bottle glasses and he was going bald.

Fierce warrior indeed. He looked as if he couldn't fight his way out of a wet paper bag. "You don't look much like a Maori to me," I said.

"Not all Maoris are big and strong," he said weedily.

Granny Nothing was disappointed too. "You don't look much like your photy, Maurice. Have you lost weight?"

"Or had a face transplant, perhaps?" I added.

Maurice didn't answer until he had taken off his glasses, given them a polish and then put them back on. "I'm afraid I have to confess. I told a little porky pie. The photograph I sent you was not of me at all."

Surprise, surprise.

Maurice went on, "I sent you a photograph of my big brother."

"Why couldn't you just have sent him instead of you?"

I was sorry I said that immediately. Little Maurice burst into tears. "Everybody prefers my brother to me. He was always the best at everything. The best rugby coach too. Just for once I wanted to be the important one. When your email came through I couldn't resist it. 'They need a Maori to save their team from humiliation,' I cried." He cried it a bit too loudly for my liking. He sounded like a halfwit. "I shall be that Maori."

"But we need a genuine rugby coach, Maurice," Granny Nothing reminded him.

"I am a genuine rugby coach. I did an internet course on the internet. How to be a rugby coach in ten easy lessons. I know all the moves." At this he started dancing about wildly. I thought he was going to fall off the platform again. He looked pleadingly at Granny Nothing. "I know I can help you. I just need somebody to give me a chance."

I expected Granny Nothing to roar at him and send him flying back on to the next train. But she never does what you expect. Instead she slapped him on the back. "I like a man with that kind of determination, Maurice." She had to grab him as he teetered on the edge. "Come on back to our place and we'll discuss tactics."

With that she lifted Maurice's case with one hand and swung it on to her shoulder. Thomas clung happily on the other.

Ewen and I followed behind them. We were feeling pretty downhearted. In fact, my heart had never been so down.

"This is the secret weapon that's going to win us the trophy?" I said. "We might as well give up now."

Granny Nothing shouted back at me, "Never give up, Stephanie darling. The words are not in my vocabulary." (She pronounced it vocalberry.) "Your Granny's got a plan."

Dad hauled open the front door before we even had the chance to knock. "Right, where is he? Where is this secret weapon?" He looked out into the street as if he was expecting him to come jogging up the road, dragging a lorry behind him with his teeth. He couldn't see Maurice. He was standing behind Granny Nothing.

"This is Maurice," she said, hauling him into view.

"This is Maurice?" Dad repeated, definitely disappointed.

"I'm stronger than I look," Maurice lied, trying to look tall.

There was a distinct smell of burning coming from inside the house. Mum had burned the authentic Maori meal, which was just as well as Maurice informed us he had a very weak stomach and Maori food disagreed with him.

"I've got a constitution like an ox, Maurice," Granny Nothing informed him. "Nothing disagrees with me."

It wouldn't dare, I thought.

So Mum boiled Maurice a couple of eggs instead.

"I still can't believe you came over here and tried to pass yourself off as your brother. You must have known we would see the difference," I asked Maurice as he ate his eggs, very daintily, I might add.

"I didn't just come over for that. I came over to meet my email girlfriend, Estelle. We've been corresponding for ages and now it's time to meet up." He showed us a picture of Estelle. She was a gorgeous blonde with long legs and scarlet lips.

"And tell me something, Maurice," Granny Nothing asked him as she studied the photograph. "Is she expecting your brother as well?"

Maurice's face went bright red. He didn't have to answer that.

"OK Maurice, say no more. I'm going to get you built up, so your lovely Estelle won't be gutted when she clocks you. Are you ready, Maurice?"

Maurice stood up and tried to look fierce. He only managed to look constipated. "Ready for anything, Granny Nothing," he said.

"Right, tomorrow we start the very first session of Granny Nothing's Fit Club."

Chapter Ten

The Singhs came over later to welcome Maurice in their own special way. I knew what that special way was as soon as I saw them with their guitars. They had composed a song in his honour. It was an Elvis Presley type of rock and roll song, and it had at least twenty verses. Every time they finished singing a verse (I use the word singing, but that's not actually what it sounded like. It sounded as if a cat had caught its tail in the tumble dryer), everyone began to clap, desperate for them to shut up. And then they would begin another monotonous verse again. Elvis had locked himself and Presley in the cupboard under the stairs and refused to let us in. "This is the fortieth time I've heard it. They've been practising for days. Find your own hiding place." And with that he slammed the door shut. Some friend.

At last, they shut up. We practically gave them a standing ovation we were so grateful.

"They like us, my dear," Mr Singh said. "Maybe we should sing another."

We couldn't get Maurice to stop applauding. "They are wonderful, aren't they," he said. "Are they professional singers?"

And he meant it.

I knew then we were dealing with an idiot.

The welcome turned into a real party. It turned out that Maurice loved a singsong. So the Singhs had run home and brought back their karaoke machine.(Did that make it a Singh song?) Mrs Scoular had turned up too. She had baked Maurice some of her fruit scones, which he refused to eat because of his stomach. She wasn't very happy about that, until Granny Nothing scoffed the lot in one go and declared them the best she'd ever tasted. After that there was no shutting Mrs Scoular up. She thought she was Kylie Minogue. Maurice thought she was brilliant as well.

"Do you think he left his brain back in New Zealand?" I wondered.

"If he ever had one," Ewen said.

"We might as well give up. We'll never win that trophy with him as the coach."

Polly turned up too. It seemed to me that half the street knew about Maurice.

"I thought Maurice was supposed to be top secret?" I said to Ewen.

"I only told Polly about him," he said.

"Trust you, Ewen," Elvis told him. "You can't keep your mouth shut about anything."

Polly grabbed him by the ears. "What did you say about Ewen?"

Elvis didn't get a chance to tell her. She jumped on him and started punching lumps out of him. Honestly, for such a tiny little thing she can be quite vicious.

There was a sudden earsplitting shriek. A Nanny Sue kind of shriek.

"Get this mutt off me!" she was yelling. Presley had her on the ground. I think he was deciding which bit of her to eat first.

That was what saved Elvis from being strangled. Polly dropped him like a dirty hankie and we all ran and dragged Presley off Nanny Sue. Wouldn't want Presley to poison himself, would we?

Nanny Sue got to her feet. She was screaming mad. She made a run for me. "What's your game?"

I jumped back. "Me? What have I done?"

She pulled something from her pocket. I thought at first it was a dirty hankie. It wasn't. It was that blinking mummy doll again.

"How did you get that into my room? Never mind, I

don't want to know." She screamed it. "I know what you're up to. You're trying to make me believe that thing's put a curse on me."

I only wish I had thought of it.

Suddenly she let out another of her bloodcurdling shrieks. "And you put another pin in it too."

She held out her hand. A little ball of blood formed on her pinkie. She threw the doll at me. I ran my finger all around it. "Well, there's no pin there now," I said.

Ewen said in his creepiest voice, "I still think it bit you."

We couldn't hold Presley any more. (Well, we weren't actually trying very hard.) He broke free and he was after her. She went off screaming at the top of her voice.

Elvis ran off after them calling for Presley, desperate to get away from Polly.

Ewen looked at me seriously. "How did it get into her room, Steph?"

"She put it there herself. You know what like she is. Always looking for attention."

"But what if it has put a curse on her?" Typical Ewen, thinking there's a mystery in everything. "We got it out of Granny Nothing's case. Remember the Shrunken Head, Steph. Remember the Rusty Key."

I refused to believe there was anything strange about them either. "Everything that happened could be explained logically. Same with this stupid doll. I'm going to put it in the garage. On the very top shelf. And we'll never see it again."

Chapter Eleven

The next day, Granny Nothing's Fit Club came into being. We came back from school (where Granny Nothing had caused havoc once again as the lollipop lady from hell) to find Maurice curled up on the sofa with a mug of tea and looking ridiculous in a pair of Mum's fluffy pink slippers. (Not that he really needed fluffy pink slippers to make him look ridiculous.) He was watching his favourite soap on television.

Granny Nothing dragged him to his feet. "Come on, Maurice, time to start working."

"Work?" He looked as if she had just asked him to climb the Himalayas.

"No time like right at this very present, Maurice. Get into your shorts."

Ewen and I had a really hard time not laughing at Maurice when we saw him in his shorts. I've never seen such knobbly knees. It didn't help that he was still wearing Mum's fluffy slippers.

"Get your trainers on, Maurice!" Granny Nothing demanded. "Try and look the part, son."

He was also wearing a vest. A string vest. Knobbly bits of bones were sticking out through the holes. He looked like a skeleton come to life.

But if Maurice was a sight to behold, he was nothing compared to Granny Nothing herself.

She was dressed in an orange T-shirt. When she's finished with it I'm sending it to a third world country as a shelter for the homeless. She was also wearing matching orange shorts.

Shorts are always a big fashion mistake for Granny Nothing. Today more than any other. The skin on her legs looks exactly the same as the skin on an orange, you know, with all those little dimply bits. Her feet were encased not so much in trainers as what looked like a couple of orange boxes. She was also wearing an orange rucksack.

The thing that scared me more than anything was . . . that I was wearing the exact same outfit.

"Aw look, sweetheart, we're twins!" She was delighted and she shook herself happily. It was only then I realized that the orange rucksack was actually Thomas strapped to her back and all dressed in orange too.

He grinned. All he had were two teeth like fangs. Honestly, he is the scariest-looking baby I have ever seen. "Twinnnnns!" he roared.

"Did you hear that! He's learned another wurrrd." Granny Nothing swung him from her back and gave him a big wet kiss. Thomas loved it, but I noticed that Maurice began to look slightly sick. "My boy is a proditchy."

Thomas was so pleased he started to yell at the top of his lungs. "Twins! Twins! Twins!" I stuck a lollipop in his mouth to shut him up. I know, we should be teaching him to eat healthily. It should have been a cauliflower or something, but I was desperate.

Ewen was all ready for his training session too. He was trying to look like David Beckham. He even had his hair tied back in a ponytail. He looked ridiculous.

Elvis crawled through the hedge. He was covered in grass and twigs. He was wearing his usual Bollywood version of shorts and T-shirt. Silk, and in a multitude of bright colours. He looked more like a mad jockey.

Presley, naturally, was there too. He was the sensible one. He came through the gate. He was dressed for his workout as well. He too wore an orange vest. I began to wonder if there had been a sale of them. Or a run on them. More appropriate for a work-out ? A run? Get it? Oh, never mind. He was also wearing a sweatband.

I mean, a dog in a sweatband, honestly.

"Can I join in, Granny Nothing?" Elvis asked.

"Course you can, son. The more the merrier."

"I go to the over-60s keep fit, can I join in?"

It was Mrs Scoular. She skipped in too, wearing what looked like a pair of navy-blue knickers. And that isn't a sight you want to see before your tea.

This was getting ridiculous, I thought.

Honestly, you don't have to be daft to live in our street, but it definitely helps.

"We're going to start with a few press-ups." Granny Nothing said.

She got down on the ground and began pushing herself up and down. It was really impressive.

"This takes me back to my days in the American Marines," she said.

"You were in the American Marines, Granny?"

Ewen believes everything. "Of course she wasn't," I whispered to him. "It's just one of her stories."

"Only part-time, but I had to leave, the sergeant fell madly in love with me, I seem to have that effect on men. Woman that look like us, Steph, have got a lot to answer for."

I almost yelled at her. "I don't look like us. I look like me."

Then she started with the sit-ups. I noticed that Maurice could manage the sit, but not the ups.

Then she had us running round the garden, jumping hurdles, which were actually upturned kitchen chairs.

Unfortunately, Maurice fell at the first chair. He grabbed his shin and rolled about like one of those footballers on the telly, pretending to be mortally injured. "I think I've broken it!" he screamed.

Granny Nothing grabbed his leg and studied it. "Rubbish, Maurice. It's just a wee dent."

But it finished Maurice for the night. We carried him back into the house and his pink fluffy slippers. I didn't know then that we were going to spend a lot of time carrying Maurice back into the house.

Chapter Twelve

It was entertainment time at our school every day. Now we relished crossing that road, all thanks to Granny Nothing.

More and more children joined us every morning. Some of them weren't even in our school. Pupils who had avoided the street and usually took seven-kilometre detours to get to school now formed a queue with us to cross the road.

A long crocodile of a queue.

Every morning the drivers went crazy as she ushered

s across the road . . . very slowly, protecting us with
,er enormous body.

"Come along, children. Take your time. Don't run.
Can't have you falling and hurting yourselves. . ." She
would turn to the motorists at that point. "Can we now?"

"I'm going to be late for work," they would shout.

"Tuff!" she would yell back.

One man, who obviously didn't know her so well,
shouted, "You want me to get out of this car and move
you, Mrs?"

She lumbered closer to his car. "Want to try it, son?"

This close he realized what he was up against. He
retreated hurriedly inside his car and rolled up his
windows.

And at home, every day we had Granny Nothing's Fit
Club Training Session. By this time, the whole of the
rugby team was turning up to join in.

"So much for our secret weapon," I moaned.

"This is brilliant. This is them getting into practice,"
Granny Nothing said. If Granny Nothing was leading
our workout, however, I didn't see why we needed
Maurice. And I said so.

Maurice burst into tears at that. Granny Nothing put
an arm around him to comfort him. "Never mind,
Maurice son. It's the very idea of having a real live
Maori here that'll send the Mini Maulers' blood racing,
that'll fire them up to win. Positive thinking, Steph.
I'm a great believer in positive thinking. Anyway,
Maurice is instructing us with the right moves."

Of course, he knew the right moves, he just couldn't actually do them.

Although, Maurice did join in the Fit Club, that is, when he was fit enough. We had discovered early that Maurice was accident prone. If something was going to happen, it would happen to Maurice. The second day, he disappeared down an open manhole during our run. Trouble was we didn't miss him for ten minutes and by the time we did we hadn't a clue where he'd gone.

Granny Nothing had us all spread out to look for him. She of course, could spread out on her own.

We called his name over and over. "Maurice! Where are you?"

Finally, we were answered by a weak cry. "Help me!"

Maurice had not only fallen down a manhole. He had managed to get himself wedged down there.

"This boy's awfy unlucky," Granny Nothing said as she hauled him free.

"This boy is an idiot," I corrected.

"I've always been accident prone," Maurice said as his knee was bandaged up.

He wasn't kidding. On the next night he tripped over a twig (a twig, mind you!) and sent himself hurtling down a hill in the park. He landed in a fast-flowing stream. He was a kilometre down-river before we caught up with him, and he needed even more bandages.

"At this rate, he's going to look like a mummy," Ewen said.

And talking about mummies, the mummy doll reappeared again.

We had just returned from one of our training sessions. Ha! Our training sessions seemed to consist mainly of carrying Maurice back to the house. Suddenly Nanny Sue lunged at Ewen and me.

Out of the dark she came like an avenging . . . well, like an avenging lunger, I suppose.

"You won't scare me with your stupid little tricks!" she screamed and she hurled something at me.

It hit me right in the kisser. The mummy doll again. "Where did you get that?" I asked her.

"Where you put it, you poisonous rat."

"I put it in the garage. Ewen saw me do it. I hope you haven't been stealing. That's breaking and entering."

"You broke into my room and left it on my pillow. That's breaking and entering, too."

"That's a lie!" I was so annoyed at her I threw the doll back at her. I was fed up looking at it. She could keep it for all I cared.

She caught it in her hand and let out another of her unearthly screams. She really should be in horror movies with a scream like that. (*Maybe I should put her in touch with Estelle*, I thought.)

"You're trying to kill me!" she cried. She held up her finger and it dripped with blood.

No. I'm exaggerating. It didn't actually drip with blood, unfortunately. But there was the tiniest spot. You could hardly see it, like a full stop on her pinkie.

"That pin's still in it!" And she threw the blinking

thing back. I examined it closely. There was nothing sticking out of it now.

I could hear Ewen catch his breath. (What a stupid idea, how do you catch your breath, in one hand?) He was sweating, and it had nothing to do with carrying Maurice.

As Nanny Sue limped back to the Singhs' cradling her wounded finger I could see the boy genius had it all figured out.

"Steph, how did it get into her room?"

I shrugged.

"And how did it bite her?"

"It didn't bite her," I reminded him. "It scratched her."

He was shaking his head. "No, it definitely bit her."

His hair was standing on end and he hadn't even gelled it.

"There is only one answer to this," he said. He paused dramatically. He should be an actor. "There is definitely a mummy's curse."

Chapter Thirteen

This time when I hid the mummy doll we decided to bury it. We buried it deep in the garden, behind the garage. Now, no one would get it from there.

"And if they do, if it turns up again in Nanny Sue's room. Then will you believe in the mummy's curse?" Ewen was convinced. I looked at my brother and, not for the first time, I thought, *The wheel is turning, but the hamster has long gone.*

I was more likely to believe that he would dig it up

himself just to convince me. Or that Nanny Sue was behind it.

Yes! How did we know she hadn't followed us, seen me hiding it in the garage and then had taken it herself? She was sneaky enough. And all that stuff about the curse and fingers dripping with blood (well, not quite dripping), all a ploy to blame Granny Nothing. She had it in for her, didn't she?

How did we know she wasn't watching us right now? I imagined her beady little eyes peering at us through next door's hedge. I looked all around. So did Ewen.

"What are you looking for, Steph?"

"Just making sure no one's watching," I said mysteriously.

"And are we going to ask Granny Nothing to tell us the secret of the mummy doll?"

I had promised him we would. "She won't tell us the truth, you know that don't you?"

"You never believe anything she says, Steph." But of course, Ewen did.

"We'll ask her," I said. "And she'll tell us a weird and wonderful tale full of magic and mystery. But I bet she picked that doll up in Mummies 'R' Us in a Glasgow market."

We planned to waylay her next day after another of her training sessions.

Mrs Scoular was loving them. "I've never felt so fit and healthy. I feel like a new woman." I think the new woman she felt like was the Bride of Frankenstein.

Maurice, on the other hand, wasn't handling it well

at all. Even before we started he dropped a weight on his head and knocked himself out. Now he had a bandage round his head to match the bandage round his legs and the ones round his knees.

When he finally regained consciousness Granny Nothing had him doing sit-ups. Suddenly he let out a yell. "I can't move. I'm stuck. It's my back. I've got a weak back," he cried.

Weak back, weak stomach, weak brain. Maurice didn't have a lot going for him. We carried him into the house still in the sitting position. "Maurice," I said to my brother, "is a bit of a muppet, isn't he?"

At that Ewen walked into the clothes pole and knocked himself out. If you ask me it's something to do with being male.

Granny Nothing looked long and hard at Maurice. "There is only one thing for it. Tomorrow, I want you to prepare yourself to be strong. There is one final thing that I can try, a last retort."

I think she meant a last resort . . . but you can never tell with Granny Nothing. Maybe she was going to hurl insults at him.

"I learned this from the tribesmen in darkest Dundee. Tomorrow we are going to try it on you, Maurice."

Maurice looked ever so slightly terrified at the prospect. Mum made him a cup of tea (weak, of course), and fetched her pink fluffy slippers for him.

"Poor little thing," she said.

This was our Secret Weapon! Thank goodness he was a secret, well, at least from the other team. We would be a laughing stock if they ever found out about him.

Granny Nothing wandered out to the garden. It had begun to rain and she had her smalls hanging on the line. Her smalls? Ha! Her knickers could be a guide to shipping, they were so massive. This was our chance. We followed her, determined to hear the story of the mummy doll.

We confessed everything to her. Told her the whole story.

"You've been in my case again . . . oh, the trouble you cause when you go in that case." She was remembering the Shrunken Head, the Rusty Key. "The mummy doll," she said mysteriously. "Oh my goodness, what a terrible thing. You have set a train of events in motion that no one can stop."

"Nanny Sue can't seem to get rid of it now," I finished.

"It's put a curse on her." Ewen insisted, hopefully. "Tell us about the mummy doll? Is it a prince of Egypt who was mummified and then shrunk?" Ewen asked. He can make up some wonderful stories himself.

"Not at all. They don't do the shrinking thing in Egypt." Granny Nothing said. "It's a strange and wonderful story," she began. She pinned Thomas up on the line while she told us. "There once was a pharaoh, and he was planning to marry a beautiful princess, Ashabulla. But the high priest, Inkibah, I think his name was, an awful nice wee man, he didn't trust Ashabulla. He was sure she was doing the dirty on her pharoah. So he watched her night and day. She hated him. So d'ye know what she did? Nasty bit of work she was.

71

Ashabulla told the pharaoh that Inkibah fancied her, and he was always trying to kiss her and everything. Well, you know what the penalty for that was?"

"He was shrunk," Ewen said. He was determined to have somebody shrunk in this story.

"I told ye, son, they don't do the shrinking thing in Egypt." She took a deep breath. "They just mummified him, alive. And they cut out his tongue! But before the last bandage got wrapped round his gob, he shouted. 'I, Inkibah, High Priest of the Temple, curse the Princess Ashabulla. I will come back. I order my followers to make a miniature mummy of me. Send it out through the wurruld, find her again. Even if it has to be in another life, I will have my vengeance, and only by confessing everything will Ashabulla be saved!'"

"This would be before his tongue got cut out presumably?" I said, rather sarcastically.

Granny Nothing gave us a wicked smile. "So if this here wee mummy keeps running after Nanny Sue it can only mean one thing ... it thinks she is the reincarnation of the beautiful princess, Ashabulla, who betrayed Inkibah. And it's out to get her."

We heard Nanny Sue shriek behind the hedge. She'd been listening to every word. I tried not to giggle as we saw her running desperately towards the Singhs' house.

"Did you know she was there?" I asked Granny Nothing.

She put on her innocent face. "Me? No? But she's going to have a hard time getting rid of that mummy doll."

"So how did it fall into your hands?" I asked her. I don't know why. I never believe a word she says.

"I was working for Ali Fez, in his wee secondhand mummy emporium in Cairo. In the Street of a Thousand Cats. Can I tell you it was the dirtiest street in the city. The smell was awful. Anyway, one day somebody brings in this wee mummy. Ali Fez nearly had a heart attack. 'AAAA! It is Inkibah! Keep it from me,' he yells. 'A thousand curses on the man who tries to sell that!'

"He got himself into an awful state. So I took it off his hands. Ali Fez says to me, 'Guard it with your life.' So I chucked it in my case, and forgot about it."

"That's your idea of guarding it with your life?" I asked her.

She had an answer for that. "I never thought I would have such nosy grandchildren. No wonder I'm always having to hide that case of mine."

"Ah, so it was you that moved it!"

She didn't answer me, she only put on that mysterious face of hers . . . or maybe she just had wind.

"Inkibah's very dirty," Ewen pointed out.

"It's a thousand years old, son. What do you expect? It's a mummy. You cannae actually chuck it in the washing machine to make it whiter than white."

Ewen was still caught up in the story. "So, there is a curse on it," he said.

Granny Nothing shook her head. "The curse is on Nanny Sue."

Chapter Fourteen

Next day, Maurice prepared himself to be strong. When Granny Nothing appeared she was wearing a gown, a mask and rubber gloves. She looked like a mad doctor about to perform an operation. "I once worked as a beautician in Vladivostok." (She pronounced it bootishun.) "I perfected there a treatment that was guaranteed to build up your muscles. I intend to use this treatment on you, Maurice, because you are a special case." I thought he was more of a head case myself. "It would take more than an ordinary treatment to build up your muscles and we're running out of time. So I have added –" she paused and we all waited expectantly – "Granny Nothing's special ingredient."

Oh no, I thought, *poor Maurice. Be afraid, Maurice. Be very afraid.*

But then, Maurice always did look afraid.

Granny Nothing's special ingredient was, as always, green. She produced a jar of green goo from beneath her gown and told Maurice to lie up on the kitchen table. I was sure Mum wouldn't be happy about that, but I said nothing. Maurice stood up, slipped on Thomas's fire engine and somersaulted on to the table.

"Clever boy, Maurice, see, my training's working already."

Maurice's eyes had crossed and there was a lump coming out on his forehead.

"Looks like he's going to need another bandage," I suggested.

Granny Nothing grinned. I always felt she was scarier-looking when she smiled. "He's going to get a lot more than one bandage."

And he did.

Granny Nothing began to cover him liberally with her green goo, and by the way, the smell was horrendous.

"Has somebody died in here?" Ewen asked, daring to sniff the jar.

"You'll get used to it," Granny Nothing told us. That

was a lie. We didn't. We ended up with pegs on our noses. The only one who seemed to enjoy the smell was Thomas, but then he can create some pretty nasty smells on his own. He sniffed the air and giggled. "Bootiful," he said.

That boy seriously worries me.

As Granny Nothing smeared the goo all over Maurice, he yelled and moaned. "I can't stand it!" he cried. His face had turned green and that had nothing to do with the goo. He just looked sick.

Granny Nothing had no sympathy at all. "Do you want to have muscles for Estelle?"

Maurice nodded.

"Do you want us to win that trophy?"

Maurice nodded again.

"Well, shut your gob."

"Shut your gob," Thomas agreed.

"I'm scared," Maurice said when Granny Nothing had left the kitchen for a moment. I almost felt sorry for him. I might even have helped him escape but he was covered in so much goo, I could never have held him. He would have skited right out of my arms. Anyway, he smelt so bad we couldn't go near him.

He was even more scared when Granny Nothing came back. She was carrying rolls and rolls of bandages.

"The theory is, Maurice," she explained as she began to wrap Maurice up. "That the ointment creates heat and the bandages keep the heat in, and the heat makes you sweat and builds up your muscles at the same time."

"Has it ever worked?" I asked her.

"I have only ever used my special ingredient once before," she said. "A puny wee guy came to the booty shop. "I want to be a famous film star," he says to me. "I want to have muscles and be strong." I took one look at him and I thought, *Well, this is a challenge for Granny Nothing.* But I covered him in my ointment and I wrapped him in the bandages and when I unwrapped him, he was built like a tank. And he went on to be one of the most famous movie stars in the business."

"And that major movie star is. . .?" I asked her.

She put a finger to her lips. "I'm sworn to secrecy. I have promised never to divulge his name. Although, actually, I can't pronounce it anyway."

Ewen's jaw dropped. "You don't mean. . ."

Honestly, Ewen is exactly like a bungalow. He has nothing upstairs.

All the time she'd been telling her story she'd been winding the bandages round and round Maurice. Finally, just as he was about to say something she put it over his mouth. He couldn't say a word. All we could see were his eyes, and they looked terrified.

Now, he really did look like a mummy.

We helped him off the table and he tried to walk. Everything was stiff, his arms, his legs, his neck. He moved in a series of spurts and lunges.

"When I take them bandages off you, Maurice, you'll have muscles like him with the funny name."

I had to admire Maurice's courage. So I didn't want to alarm him any further, but it did occur to me that he was going to have a lot of trouble when he wanted to go to the toilet.

Chapter Fifteen

After a couple of hours the heat was getting to Maurice. "I'm on fire!" he shouted.

Granny Nothing gave him a drink of cold water through a straw.

"That means it's working," she told him.

"I'm burning up," he yelled.

After a while we got fed up listening to him, and wrapped more bandages round his mouth. Then we left him in the conservatory alone.

"He really is a moan," I said to Ewen.

"I'm going out to cool down," we heard him mumble. We ignored that too. Let him strut about in the garden. What harm could he come to there?

He was only out ten minutes when we heard a bloodcurdling shriek. We recognized the sound immediately. It could only have been made by one person. Nanny Sue.

"Agh! The mummy has come alive to get me!" she was screaming.

Ewen and I ran outside. Maurice was advancing on Nanny Sue, his arms outstretched. He was probably trying to explain who he was, but it's hard to talk when your mouth's bandaged up.

He was muttering and mumbling like someone whose tongue's been cut out.

We tried to explain it was only Maurice, but she wouldn't listen. "I heard her story. I am the reincarnation of that beautiful princess and Inkibah has come back to wreak revenge on me."

Honestly, her, a beautiful princess? In her dreams.

"Get away from me! I am your mistress, Ashabulla. I command it."

Maurice just kept advancing on her, mumbling.

Nanny Sue was almost hysterical. "How do I get this curse off me? Why was I born so beautiful?"

It was actually turning into a very entertaining spectacle. We called on Elvis and Presley to come and watch. I suppose we should have led Maurice away, calmed her down, explained everything, and we did discuss it. We even had a vote on it. A show of hands, or a show of paws in Presley's case. But I'm afraid the vote went against her. She finally backed so far against the hedge, she had nowhere else to go. She crumpled in a heap in the corner of the garden. That's when we took our chance and brought Maurice back into the house. We had him hidden in his room by the time Nanny Sue regained consciousness. She stood up shakily and she was pale with anger. "She did this!" she cried. "Granny Nothing did this! She's put a curse on me. But I'll make her sorry. You wait and see. Vengeance shall be mine!" Then she turned and ran back to the Singhs'.

Granny Nothing stuck her head out the bedroom window. "What rattled her chain?" she asked.

That night we all stood by to watch the Great Unwrapping. Mum had lit candles and they gave off an eerie glow which added to the occasion. There was an atmosphere of mystery about the place, or there would have been if it hadn't been for the smell. It kind of took away from the air of mystery with us all wearing clothes pegs on our noses.

"This is just like Christmas," Ewen said. "When you unwrap your presents and you don't know what you're getting."

He wasn't wrong there. We didn't know what we were going to get. Would Maurice now have muscles like Arnold Scwar . . . Swatzer . . . Shottsin . . . him with the funny name? Or would he still be Maurice the Muppet?

Everyone held their breath, and their nose. I could hardly bear to look. All we needed was a drum roll and the occasion would be complete.

The last bandage was removed. We all gasped.

Maurice. . .

Hadn't changed a bit. Except now he was dyed green.

Granny Nothing was disappointed. "I don't understand it," she said. "Maybe he just needs another coat."

"You could put a hundred coats on him, and a couple of blankets and it wouldn't make any difference. Nothing's going to work on him," I told her.

"I'm sorry," Maurice whimpered. "I've let you all down. And Estelle's coming tomorrow and I'm going to let her down too. I'm not what she was expecting either."

Especially now, I thought, that he was green.

Chapter Sixteen

That night Ewen and I found Maurice sitting in his room looking forlorn. He was staring wistfully at a photograph of the beautiful Estelle.

"I'm going to be such a disappointment to her," he said. "She's expecting a big handsome Maori, and what does she get? Me. And I'm green."

Actually, I thought the green was an improvement. It gave him a bit of colour.

I sat down beside him. I really wanted to cheer the little soul up. He'd had a bad day. "Look, Maurice, how do you know that Estelle will look like her photo? You sent one of your handsome brother. Maybe she sent one of her beautiful sister."

His eyes lit up with hope. "You think so?"

I did more than think so. I mean, let's face it, what would a gorgeous female like the one in the photo be doing looking for a man on the internet? She'd have men swarming over her, surely?

"Take my word for it, Maurice," I assured him. "You look for the ugliest girl that steps off that train tomorrow and that will be your Estelle."

He glowed. But then, that might have been the green tinge. "Oh, that would make me so happy," he said.

We all stood waiting for the train to pull in to the station. Maurice had had three baths and two showers, but he was still green. Granny Nothing kept telling him that all that water was bad for him. He was dressed up in his best suit. He even had a flower in his buttonhole. Unfortunately it was a daffodil, which kind of clashed with the green.

The train came to a halt and people started spilling on to the platform. There was a gentleman in a bowler hat, carrying a briefcase. He looked all around, as if he was expecting someone to meet him.

"Do you think that might be Estelle?" Ewen asked. As I have said on many occasions, my brother's lift does not go to the top floor.

A little old lady was having trouble with her zimmer. I just hoped *she* wasn't Estelle.

Then a female, I think she was a female, with beer-bottle glasses tripped out of a carriage and landed face down on the platform. I nudged Maurice. "What did I tell you, Maurice. There's your Estelle."

He looked genuinely happy. Because, let's face it, he couldn't possibly disappoint this female. She was so ugly, she would be glad of any man, surely? Anyway, with glasses like that she probably couldn't see a thing.

We all hurried to help her to her feet. But we were too late.

Someone else was already there. Scarlet-nailed fingers were clasping the girl's arms gently as she was helped to her feet. The fingers belonged to slender hands and the hands were attached to a body to die for.

Estelle!

I could feel Maurice freeze beside me.

She looked exactly like her photograph. No, not exactly. The real thing was even more gorgeous. This was the beautiful Estelle.

She looked beyond us as if we weren't there. She was looking towards the entrance to the station, looking for the handsome, muscle-bound Maori she had been promised. And all we had to offer was Maurice.

She took a step back when she saw him approaching her. She probably thought the aliens had landed. She would be convinced of it when she caught sight of Granny Nothing. She bounded along the platform with Thomas curled on her head like a fur hat. Granny

Nothing wasted no time. She came right out with it. "Are you Estelle, darlin'?" she asked.

Estelle looked scared. The first sight of Granny Nothing does that to people. She nodded.

"Well," Granny Nothing went on. "I hate to be the bringer of bad news but. . ." At this point she put her hand on Maurice's shoulder. I think she was actually holding him up. "But this is the Maurice you were expecting."

Estelle looked at Maurice.

Maurice looked sick.

"I'm sorry, Estelle," he began to apologize.

Suddenly, the beautiful Estelle leaped at him and covered him in kisses., "Oh Maurice darling. I hope I'm not a disappointment to you."

Maurice was literally lost for words. Words were hiding in the bushes, and he couldn't find them anywhere. So I said it for him. "He was thinking the same thing, actually. He's lost a bit of weight since he sent you that photograph."

Estelle hugged him tightly. "Oh Maurice, I don't care about that. It wasn't your photograph I fell in love with. It was your beautiful letters. They were sheer poetry."

Now I had seen some of Maurice's email letters to Estelle.

Hi, how are you? I am fine. It is raining here. Is it raining there also?

She fell in love with that!

All at once, he was hugging her back. "Oh Estelle, my darling!" he said.

"Maurice, my love," she said.

"Yuch," I said.

When we got home the Singhs were there to welcome Estelle. And they had their guitars with them. They had composed a welcome song for Estelle, and this one had forty verses.

Ewen and I tried to hide in the cupboard under the stairs, but Elvis and Presley were already there and refused to let us in, again.

When the Singhs' song was finished (and that must have been midnight), Estelle clapped enthusiastically. "Oh, that was wonderful!" she said. "Are you two professionals?"

I knew then that Maurice had met his perfect match. One was as daft as the other.

Chapter Seventeen

It was the morning of the second leg of the rugby final. And Maurice still didn't have any muscles. "We might as well give this up," I said to Ewen. "We're never going to win."

However, Granny Nothing had a plan.

That morning at breakfast she brought a box into the kitchen. We all waited to see what was in the box. She ripped it open and pulled out . . . a big roll of foam.

"What on earth is that?" we all asked at once.

"It's an Incredible Hulk suit," she grinned. "Me and

Estelle got together and she had this sent from the film studio where she works."

Estelle was excited. "We're going to put Maurice in this. And I'm going to make him up to look really fierce." She smiled. "I'm going to use the same make-up I used on *Zombie Killer Cannibals from Hell*."

Ewen was so impressed he almost fell off his seat. *Zombie Killer Cannibals from Hell* was his favourite film . . . or it would be if he was ever allowed to watch it.

We all sat in the living room and waited for the magic transformation of Maurice. It took them over an hour, and then the finished version stepped into the living room. I say stepped, but in the Hulk suit it was more like a roll.

"Very impressive," Dad said.

"Oh yes it is," Mum said.

"It's different," sang the Singhs.

"But does he look scary?" Estelle asked.

Ewen was the only one brave enough to tell the truth. "He looks like a muppet," he said.

Thomas agreed. "Muuuuuppet!" he roared.

Personally, I thought Maurice just looked stupid. Now he had indeed a very muscular body, but nothing could disguise his tiny wee head. Estelle had done a wonderful job on his face. He even had skin falling off and everything. How had she managed that? I wondered. But he was still wearing his thick beer-bottle glasses, and it didn't help either that he had on Mum's fluffy pink slippers.

He took a step towards us and let out a whimper. I think he was trying to frighten us. And he fell flat on his face.

"It's never going to work!" he cried pitifully. "I told them. It's never going to work."

Granny Nothing sighed. "You might be right, Maurice. I think there's only one thing for it."

"We just don't turn up?" Ewen suggested.

Granny Nothing bellowed with laughter. "No, son. I think we'll just have to cheat."

Thomas laughed too. "Cheat!" he repeated.

In fact we were all laughing.

Just then I saw a movement at the window.

It was Nanny Sue, and she had heard everything.

When our team arrived at the school rugby field the Burrington Bears were already there. They were standing round their bus having a team talk with Coach Muldoon. "Can't we go back in the dressing room?" They were all moaning. "It's time we changed into our kits for the game." They were obviously anxious to slaughter us once again.

"In a minute, boys!" Coach Muldoon shouted.

Right at that moment Coach Muldoon noticed Maurice, the slightly incredible Hulk. His lips began to quiver, he started to giggle. "Do you see what I see boys?" He pointed at Maurice. Maurice's little head disappeared inside his Hulk suit. "I think he thinks it's Halloween. What do you bet, boys?" And then they all started to laugh. Pointing their fingers and making a fool of poor old Maurice. I felt like kicking the lot of them.

Granny Nothing stood in front of him. "You leave this boy be, or Granny Nothing'll make you sorry." Her whole body was quivering. "Shut your gobs!" she roared.

And they did. But only until we had all made our way to our team dressing room. Then we could distinctly hear them laughing and cackling, while Coach Muldoon made bets about who could mimic Maurice the best.

"I've let you all down," Maurice said, slumping down on a bench, and then rolling off on to the floor. "I'm a failure."

Granny Nothing lifted him to his feet. "Never give up, Maurice. We can win, I know we can." Then she went off to organize the cheerleaders.

The Mini Maulers were as despondent as Maurice. Most of them didn't see any point in playing at all.

Polly tried to cheer them up. "With Ewen on the team you stand a really good chance of winning."

Elvis began to laugh. She had cheered him up, anyway. But only for a moment.

"What's so funny?" Polly asked through gritted teeth, a dangerous sign.

Elvis didn't spot it. "Ewen? A really good chance with him on the team? Come on, we'd be better off with Presley playing the match."

He hardly had the words out. Polly leaped at him. She sent him sprawling and before he had a chance to stand up she was on top of him. I began to think we would be better with Polly on the team. She could thump the Burrington Bears into submission.

"Ewen's wonderful!" Polly yelled at him. Ewen looked around proudly, but then he thinks he's wonderful anyway.

Polly was trying to strangle Elvis, and we were all standing round enjoying the spectacle, for a moment the match the furthest thing from our minds. Until, that is, the door of the dressing room banged open. Nanny Sue was standing there, her mouth open, her eyes wide. I ducked, sure the mummy doll was about to be flung in my face again. But no. She screamed dramatically, "Come and see this! You all have to come and see this!"

So we all came, the Mini Maulers, Mum and Dad, Mrs Scoular, Baldy, the Singhs. Even Coach Muldoon and the Bears were there. Nanny Sue had gathered everyone together. She stopped at the Burrington Bears' dressing room.

"Look at this!" And she flung the door open with a flourish.

We were all too stunned to say a word.

Granny Nothing was in the dressing room. She had a can of itching powder in her hands, and it looked like she was putting it into the Burrington Bears' shorts.

Chapter Eighteen

"I heard her!" Nanny Sue told everyone. "I heard her say she was going to cheat so her team could win."

Granny Nothing shouted back. "I've never cheated in my life. And I'll thump anybody that says I have."

Dad stepped forward. "My mother would never cheat. There has to be another explanation."

Thomas shook his head wildly in agreement.

Mum put her hand gently on Granny Nothing's shoulders. "I don't believe she would cheat either."

Granny Nothing grinned at her. "Och, thank you, sweetheart."

Even Baldy stepped forward in her defence. "I'm sure if she has put itching powder in the team's shorts she had a good reason."

Somehow I don't think that really helped her that much.

"I did not put itching powder in them shorts!"

"You were caught red-handed!" Nanny Sue said triumphantly.

"I got a message to come here," Granny Nothing roared. "It said there was something fishy going on and I was the only one who could stop it. I came in here and found this can of itching powder and—"

"A likely story," Nanny Sue snapped.

The Burrington Bears were going wild. "You said 'Granny Nothing'll get ye!' You said we'd be sorry!"

Granny Nothing looked around at everyone else, our friends, our neighbours. "Do you really think I did this?"

Their eyes moved to the floor. No one could face her. They didn't blame her. They didn't even accuse her. They were all sure she had done it with the best of intentions. But they believed she had done it anyway.

"It's just not the way we do things around here," Mrs Scoular sniffed.

Baldy turned to Coach Muldoon. "Under the circumstances I believe we will have to forfeit the match. Your team naturally will take home the trophy."

To my surprise Coach Muldoon protested loudly.

"No. We refuse to accept. We'll play the match another day."

"No. I insist," Baldy, well, insisted really.

"I speak on behalf of the whole team. We refuse to accept," Coach Muldoon said.

"No, we don't!" the whole team called out as one.

"You don't want to win like this," Coach Muldoon appealed to their better nature.

"Yes, we do!" they shouted back. Obviously none of them had a better nature.

So they were handed the trophy, without much ceremony, and not a lot of cheering. Even Coach Muldoon looked unhappy.

And Thomas started crying, and that can only ever mean one thing. He couldn't see his beloved Granny Nothing. It was only then I noticed that there was no sign of her. She must have gone home, I supposed.

It was a miserable journey back to the house.

"I don't know who cheated, but it wasn't my mother," Dad kept saying.

I knew he was right. There had to be another explanation. But what was it? Had Granny Nothing been framed? And who would possibly want to frame her?

One name leaped into my mind. In fact it didn't leap, it somersaulted. Nanny Sue. She was the only one who skipped home happily, humming her favourite tune, off key.

Nanny Sue had sworn vengeance on Granny Nothing. Now she looked smug. I pulled Ewen and Elvis aside. "I bet it was Nanny Sue who did this."

Presley must have understood. He started snarling, and growling. Nanny Sue heard him and she turned slowly round. "Keep that mutt away from me!" she shouted.

But it was too late. Presley was after her. She screeched and began to run, leaping over the hedges like an Olympic athlete.

Mrs Singh sighed. "She's a wonderful girl really. Even at a sad time like this she's ready to play with Presley."

We couldn't get Thomas to shut up. "We'll be home soon, Thomas," Mum kept telling him. "And your Granny will be there."

As we went up the path to our house Dad warned us not to mention a thing about the match. "We just act as if nothing had happened. Right?"

"Right!" we agreed.

The Singhs offered to bring over their karaoke machine and because we were desperate we agreed. Maurice and Estelle said they would treat her to a tango. (Whatever that was.)

But when we got into the house, there was no sign of Granny Nothing.

Ewen and I ran up to her room. Her clothes weren't in her wardrobe.

The only thing that was left of her was that interesting smell.

Granny Nothing had gone.

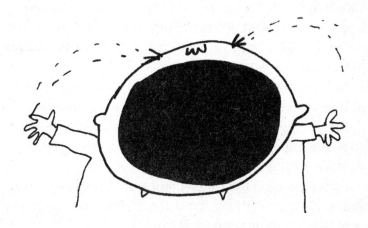

Chapter Nineteen

Thomas wailed even louder, as if he knew that she hadn't just popped into the toilet and would be out when she finished reading the paper. As if he knew that she hadn't just pushed him into someone's arms with a wild cry of, "Hold my boy!" while she went off to save the wurruld.

It looked as if she would never cry, "Hold my boy!" again. Dad hunted everywhere for her. In the garage, in the loft, down in the cellar. But she had gone.

"It's my fault," he said. "I should have told her we'd find out the truth."

"No. It's my fault," Mum said. "I should have told her it didn't matter whether she was guilty or not, we'd still love her."

"It's my fault," Maurice said. "If I'd been a big strong boy like my brother she wouldn't have had to put itching powder in those shorts. We could have won fair and square."

"It's my fault," said Estelle. "If I'd been better at making Maurice look fierce, more like a Zombie Killer Cannibal from Hell, he would have scared the life out of that team and she wouldn't have had to cheat."

"She did not cheat!" I shouted.

"She'd never cheat!" Ewen and Elvis and Dad shouted at the same time.

"Grrrrrrr," agreed Thomas.

Even Presley paused for a moment chasing Nanny Sue and let out a plaintive wail.

"She did cheat!" Nanny Sue shouted. And we all chased her.

Next day at school everyone was miserable. And it wasn't just because we'd lost the final. Everyone missed Granny Nothing.

Mrs Bradley was back from sick leave, and was almost sick again when she heard about Granny Nothing. "That woman saved my life. She would never cheat!" and she cried so much we had to help her into the office for a cup of tea. To be honest anyway, we didn't need a lollipop lady to help us across the street any more. None of the cars used our street as a shortcut to the motorway now. Granny Nothing had seen to that. And the cars that did drive along the street travelled in a leisurely crawl, insisting we take our time crossing the road.

Todd Dangerfield started a petition to say none of us believed she'd been cheating. She'd been framed.

"Granny Nothing would never do anything underhand!" he told everyone as they signed.

Todd Dangerfield, once our arch-enemy and the biggest bully in the school, was now the gentlest boy you could ever meet.

"And I'll thump anybody who doesn't sign," he added.

He was a bully no more, thanks to Granny Nothing.

She had changed all our lives, made life interesting, and now she was gone.

Baldy called the whole school into morning assembly. "I have heard that Granny Nothing has gone and we are all going to miss her terribly."

Funny, but he looked rather pleased about it.

"Who is he trying to kid?" I said to Ewen. "He's glad to get rid of her. He's terrified of Granny Nothing."

"But you know," Baldy went on. "This should teach us all a valuable lesson. Nothing is worth while if you have to cheat to get it. Granny Nothing should not have cheated."

Well, the hall went wild.

"No! She didn't," I yelled.

The chant was taken up by us all.

"No! She didn't! No! She didn't!"

"Yes, she did!" Baldy tried to make himself heard above the din. "She was caught red-handed."

"She was framed!" we all yelled.

I turned to Ewen. "We have to do something to prove it was Nanny Sue who put that itching powder in the shorts. But how?"

Ewen suggested kidnapping and torture, but I drew the line at that. *If only,* I thought, *we could trick her into telling us everything...*

Then it came to me. The perfect solution. Why am I so clever? No one should have as much brains as me.

"I know exactly how," I said. "We are going to scare her into confessing."

Chapter Twenty

I love the dark nights when the clocks go back and an air of mystery seems to hang about the streets. We'd never have been able to scare Nanny Sue in daylight, but in the dark when every shadow would make her shriek, we could sure scare her then.

Everyone wanted to help when we told them my plan. And it was a simple one. Nanny Sue was convinced there was a curse on her. A mummy's curse. We were going to dress up as mummies and scare the living daylights out of her.

Todd bought up the local supermarket's whole stock of bandages. He assured them he had joined the junior Red Cross and was going after his bandaging badge. They didn't believe him. Todd's reputation as a bully still hung around him like a bad smell.

"Are you sure these aren't to bandage up your next victims?" the staff asked him.

"It's not fair," Todd moaned. "I'm trying to turn over a new leaf." But he'll have to keep working to convince people about that.

We had a great time wrapping ourselves up in the bandages, and when we ran out of bandages, we used toilet rolls. Estelle was a great help. We asked her to make us look really scary and told her that Baldy had decided the school play should be *Mummy Killer Cannibals from Hell*.

She believed us. Which goes to prove she's just as much of an idiot as Maurice. But nice with it.

However, I have to say when she'd finished we did look scary. But not scary enough for Estelle.

"Why don't you hang a torch around your neck upside down?" The torch, not our necks. "It'll look like an Egyptian necklet, and when you turn it on the light will shine up into your faces. They'll look even scarier."

She was right about that. The light gave our faces an eerie glow.

"Right," I said when we were ready. "Now before we go, I'm in charge here. Do whatever I do."

Elvis went loopy. "It's my garden we're going into. I'm in charge."

Polly butted in. "I think Ewen should be in charge."

"Him?" Elvis said. "He's thick as a brick."

Elvis would never learn. Polly leaped on him and tried to unwrap him. "Take that back!"

We had to pull her off him and by that time their bandages were entwined and it took ages to separate them.

"It was my idea!" I said angrily. It would be daylight before we did anything at this rate. "I'm in charge."

"No. I want to be the chief mummy. It's my garden!" Elvis said.

"Oh, let him be in charge, Steph!" Ewen said. "Let's get on with it."

I finally had to give in. Very reluctantly, I might add. We staggered out into the night. Arms outstretched, walking like, well, hopefully, like mummies. We climbed through the hedge into the Singhs' garden, and as Elvis led us to Nanny Sue's window we all began to moan and cry out for vengeance. Personally I thought it was a mistake to bandage Presley. I mean, who ever heard of a mummy dog? But Elvis refused to go without him. So he staggered along with us, bandaged from head to paws.

"Nanny Sue," we chanted through the dark. "Nanny Sue. . ."

For a moment I was sure we had gone a bit too far. She was bound to see through the whole thing. It would never work. A group of wailing mini-mummies and a mummy dog? Come on, you would have to be an idiot to fall for that.

But of course, I forgot we were dealing with Nanny Sue here, whose brain was removed at birth.

She came to her window. She peered through the glass, trying to make us out in the dark and then she slid up her window.

That was when we all switched on our torches.

Here eyes went wide. What did she see? An army of mummies advancing on her, eerie lights illuminating their faces as they chanted over and over, "Nanny Sue. Nanny Sue."

She let out a strangled cry. She screamed.

I just hoped the Singhs wouldn't be alerted, but they were practising a wedding song for Maurice and Estelle (she had proposed while he was still wearing his zombie make-up, which just goes to prove love really is blind). Anyway, the Singhs were oblivious to any other strange noises.

"They've come for me!" Nanny Sue screamed. "Please, go away. I am not the reincarnation of your beautiful princess. I did not betray you. It must have been another beautiful Nanny Sue. I am innocent."

Still we kept moaning and advancing on her.

"You are not innocent," I cried hoarsely, trying to make my voice sound fierce. "You lied about Granny Nothing."

She let out another of her moans.

"Confess everything and we will leave you alone," I chanted in what I hoped was a scary tone. It certainly scared Nanny Sue.

"I have nothing to confess, I tell you."

"You lied about Granny Nothing. You said she cheated and you know she didn't."

She looked even more terrified this close up. "How did you know?" she cried.

"Because . . . I am the mummy, Inkibah," I cried.

Elvis kicked me. "I am Inkibah."

Ewen joined in. "I am Inkibah."

Soon all the mummies were chanting the same thing. "I am Inkibah."

I felt like yelling. Here she was ready to confess and they were going to ruin everything, making us all sound ridiculous.

"I'll confess," she cried out finally.

We all held our breath. We had done it. She was about to admit that she was the one who had put the itching powder in the shorts.

But she didn't.

In fact, she took us all by surprise.

"It was Coach Muldoon who did it. And I've got the CCTV footage to prove it!"

Chapter Twenty-one

So, there it was.

As soon as she said it Nanny Sue disappeared from the window in a faint.

All us mummies looked at each other. Coach Muldoon?

I pulled the bandages from my mouth. "That's why he didn't want to take the trophy."

"He didn't want his team to win?" Ewen was baffled. "But why?"

I couldn't understand that either, but when we ran in

to the house and told Dad what Nanny Sue had said, he understood right away. "Coach Muldoon is a betting man. He would bet on anything. His team were the favourites, so if he bet on the Mini Maulers and we won, he would win a lot of money."

"But how did you get Nanny Sue to confess?" Mum asked us.

By that time, of course, I was no longer a mummy. I was, once again, the beautiful Stephanie. "We were playing in the garden, and we overheard her. She must have been talking to herself. She's been acting very strange lately."

I didn't add that she'd been acting very strange all her life.

Dad nodded his head. "Guilt," he said. "Guilt can make people do funny things."

After that everyone went to the Singhs' to confront Nanny Sue.

Mrs Singh was genuinely worried about her. "I think she needs a holiday. She's just not been herself lately."

I wished that were true. Any other self would be an improvement on Nanny Sue.

Mrs Singh knocked politely on Nanny Sue's door.

Nanny Sue shouted, "Get away. I am not the reincarnation of your beautiful princess. I did not betray you!"

Mrs Singh looked around at us. "She's hallucinating," she said.

Dad called through the door next. He told her he

knew everything. He wanted her to hand over the CCTV footage to clear Granny Nothing.

Nanny Sue pulled open the door. Her hair was standing on end and she looked as if she'd been hiding under the bed. "The mummies told you, didn't they?"

We all tried not to giggle. Mrs Singh touched her head. "She's not right," she mouthed. "She does need a holiday."

Nanny Sue threw the tape at us and slammed the door shut, but not before Presley had leaped through and into the room with her. The last we heard was her strangled scream.

"Presley just loves her," Mr Singh said. "He'll cheer her up."

Dad held the tape in his hand. "I'll take this to the school rugby board right away. This will mean a rematch, of course."

A rematch? What would be the point of that? We'd still lose.

When we got back to the house I knew something was different. Had we been broken into? There were strange noises coming from upstairs, and a revolting, but familiar smell wafting through the house.

And, most telling of all, Thomas stopped crying.

Granny Nothing was back.

Chapter Twenty-two

I thought for a moment Thomas was about to walk, that he was going to take his first independent steps in his eagerness to reach his Granny. He threw himself from Mum's arms and stood on the bottom step, on his own, not holding on to anything and he let out a screech. "Grrrrranny!"

Then, just when we thought he was about to walk, he dropped to his knees and he was up those stairs as if he was on an escalator.

Granny Nothing met him halfway. "My boy!" she

cried, thundering down to lift him into her arms.

"Mum!" Dad shouted. "I'm so glad you're back. Where have you been?" I'm sure there was a tear in Dad's eye.

"I'll tell you later, son," she answered. She held Thomas high in the air, letting him dribble all over her. "My boy!" she said again.

Dad showed her the tape. "You were framed," he said. "It was Coach Muldoon who put that itching powder in the shorts. And Nanny Sue saw him and she stole this tape so she could blame you."

"She sent you the message too, so you would be in the dressing room with the itching powder just when we all arrived to see you," Mum said. "But don't be too hard on her." Why is my Mum always so soft! "I don't think she's right in the head."

"She won't be when I'm finished with her," Granny Nothing roared.

Mum and Dad went off to make some celebration tea and Ewen and I followed Granny Nothing into her bedroom. It was comforting to see her clothes lying about again. Her massive tights draped over the chair, her case peeking out from just under her bed. (Her case! Now we knew where it had gone to.) Thomas couldn't get close enough to her. He was clinging on to her neck, kissing her, licking her, biting her, loving her.

"So why did you run away?" I asked her. "Just because some people thought you had cheated?"

"We knew you weren't guilty, Granny." Ewen told her. "All of the children knew, that's why we dressed up as mummies and frightened Nanny Sue into confessing."

Granny Nothing smiled at us. "That was a lovely thing you did. Lovely. Having all that faith in Granny Nothing."

She still hadn't answered our question. "So, where did you go?" I asked her. "To that little bed and breakfast in the High Street?"

Her eyes darted from side to side. She put a finger to her lips. She peeked out the window as if she was making sure no one was hanging on the sill by their fingertips listening to her. Then she closed the bedroom door very quietly. "Didn't I tell you I might get the call at a moment's notice? That I would not be able to divulge where I was going to anybody? I told you I signed the Fishul Secrets Act."

Here we go again, I thought. "So, you are trying to say you were off on a mission?"

"Exactly," she said.

"And how did you get this call? By carrier pigeon?"

She shook her head. Thomas fell off and she caught him deftly. "Coded text message," she said. "They needed me desperately in one of the trouble spots of the wurruld. Hostages had been taken. I was the only one who could get them oot. They flew me in and dropped me by heliocopter –" yes, she pronounced it heliocopter – "in the dead of night. No one was to know I was there. I went undercover. I had to rescue them hostages and then nip out again, smartish." She stood tall and proud, with Thomas balanced in her hand like an Oscar. "My country needed me, and I

111

answered the call. The Secret Weapon saves the wurruld again!"

What a load of twaddle she talks. Does she honestly think we'd believe a story like that?

"Oh, Granny, you're so brave. Can you teach me to be a Secret Weapon?" I might have known Ewen, my daft brother, would be completely taken in.

"You'd need a brain transplant first," I told him.

"I will teach you all I know, son. But remember, this is between us. Our secret. No one must ever find out the truth." She opened the door and peeked out. "So I'll just tell your dad I went to his auntie's in Aberdeen."

Chapter Twenty-three

The day of the rematch dawned bright and clear. Everyone turned up to watch us lose again. We certainly had the most pitiful bunch of cheerleaders. Granny Nothing had now been joined by Mrs Scoular. "After those training sessions I've got the body of a twenty year old!" she said.

Well, it was the scrawniest-looking twenty year old body I'd ever seen.

I would have offered to be a cheerleader myself, but

Polly told me I had two left feet and she took my place instead. Little show-off.

Granny Nothing and Maurice were giving our team a pre-match talking-to in the dressing room. Todd slumped along the bench. "What's the point of this? We're going to lose the match anyway."

"That's not positive thinking, Todd," Granny Nothing told him. "You're going out there, and you are going to win that trophy . . . and I'm going to tell you how you're going to do it."

"Tie the other team's shoelaces together?" Todd suggested.

Granny Nothing ignored him. "You are going to roar your way to victory."

"Did you say . . . roar?" Ewen asked.

"Aye. Roar. See when the Scottish soldiers –" she pronounced it sojers – "go into battle with their kilts swinging and their bagpipes playing, they scare the living daylights out of the enemy, and do you know how they do it?"

"Yes," I said. "The noise of the bagpipes will do it every time."

Everyone laughed except Granny Nothing.

"It's the roar that does it. They roar their way into battle and it's clean underwear time for the enemy."

"You're going to teach them to roar like a Scottish sojer . . . I mean, soldier?" Maurice asked.

She walloped him on the back and almost sent him flying across the room. "No, Maurice. You're going to teach them to roar like a Maori. The Maoris have the best roar in the world. The haka." Suddenly, her eyes went wide as saucers. Her tongue started waggling about in her mouth. She looked demented. And then she roared. She roared so loud I thought my eardrums were about to burst.

"You, Maurice my boy, are going to teach this team a haka to die for."

Our team was late coming on to the field. "What's keeping them?" the referee asked, looking at his watch.

We all pretended we didn't know, but, of course, they were learning the haka. But, would it help?

At last they came out. Estelle had obviously been at them too, for their faces were streaked and daubed with make-up. They looked exactly like Zombie Killer Cannibals from Hell. (If you ask me that's the only film Estelle has worked on.)

"Oh look, they're wearing make-up!" one of the Burrington Bears shouted. And they all laughed and pointed. I could see this was getting the Mini Maulers' backs up.

Before the game began, the visiting team sang their school song. Something about gathering round the campfire with their wonderful headmaster, and eating their school dinners and enjoying them.

It was pitiful.

Then it was the Mini Maulers' turn.

They went into action.

They crouched. They stamped their feet. And they began to roar.

"Kamate Kamate
Kaora Kaora
Tenete Tangata
Tuhuri Tuhuri."

As they roared the haka they stamped towards the other team, advancing step by step. They took the Burrington Bears by surprise. They all stepped back.

The Maulers' eyes were wide, their tongues waggling about like live serpents in their mouths. Suddenly the make-up the Bears had laughed at had turned into warpaint, and the Bears were scared. I could see it in their faces.

The crowd got into the swing of it too.

They started singing the haka.

"Kamate Kamate
Kaora Kaora
Tenete Tangata
Tuhuri Tuhuri."

It rang around the stands, encircling the Bears like an ambush.

Granny Nothing was right. That haka made them lose their confidence completely. When the game began, the Bears kept glancing round as if they thought the Maulers were going to rush them. In a scrum they couldn't concentrate, watching for the Maulers advancing. They were caught every time they tried to make a run, and it was the roar that did it. Even

Ewen, the most useless man on the field, had them running scared. Of course it helped that he had his tongue waggling about wildly the whole game.

By half time the score was. . .

Oh, I never understand rugby scores. We were winning anyway.

By full time, we had trounced them!

The supporters went wild.

Polly ran on to the field. "Wasn't he wonderful, Steph? Wasn't he just wonderful?"

I thought my brother had been the worst player on the team, but I suppose love is blind so I didn't say that to Polly.

She screamed with delight and ran towards him.

And ran right past him.

She threw her arms around Elvis. He tried to defend himself, sure she was about to attack him again.

"Oh, Elvis, you were wonderful."

Ewen's mouth was hanging open. In fact, it almost hit the ground. "What is she telling Elvis he's wonderful for? I'm the one she thinks is wonderful."

"Women are fickle, Ewen," I told him. "I think she's turned her attentions to Elvis now. But I thought you didn't like her anyway?"

"No. I don't. I don't care. Doesn't bother me."

But he couldn't take his eyes off them anyway.

Maurice was lifted high on the team's shoulders. He was almost in tears. At last he'd beaten his brother, and got the girl. Estelle blew him kisses. Our Secret Weapon had come through at last.

Our other Secret Weapon, Granny Nothing, was being showered with praise too.

"You're wonderful!" the Singhs sang.

"You're brilliant," Dad shouted.

"You're quite nice!" Mrs Scoular said.

Baldy's big mistake was suggesting they lift Granny Nothing shoulder high. Without a crane? Was the man mad?

Of course he was. Which was why we all spent the rest of the day being bandaged up in Casualty.

Chapter Twenty-four

The day of Maurice and Estelle's wedding dawned bright and clear. No. It didn't. Actually, it poured. But nothing could put a damper on their happiness. Estelle was the most beautiful bride I had ever seen.

Honestly.

I couldn't think why she was marrying the weedy Maurice, until she said, "Isn't he the handsomest man in the world?"

This was Maurice, who still had a definite tinge of green.

I remembered then she was as daft as a brush. (How daft is a brush?) But nice with it.

There were some wonderful outfits at the wedding. The Singhs wore their matching diamante Elvis Presley suits. We all had to wear sunglasses to look at them. Elvis strode in magnificently dressed like a Bollywood version of a maharajah. He wore a kaftan of gold. Presley marched beside him in a matching gold turban.

Then, Polly arrived in a sari and made a beeline for Elvis. As soon as he saw her Elvis jumped on Presley's back and galloped back into his own garden.

Mrs Scoular wore a backless Kylie Minogue type of minidress. Unfortunately, she wore it back to front. Nobody noticed.

Baldy just looked like another mummy. He had suffered the most damage trying to lift Granny Nothing, and he was still in bandages.

Granny Nothing turned up looking like a pink meringue. Her hat was a pink fluff on her head. Or . . . was that Thomas?

No. It was definitely her hat.

Her dress was like a pink mini ballgown. It was short (to show off those lovely legs) and she had a matching pink bag. From the shape of it I think she had a machine gun in there. Thomas was tucked into a pocket in the front of her dress. He looked like a dribbling baby kangaroo in a kilt. Yes. A kilt. He even had a set of bagpipes. He blew into them all through the reception and made the most horrendous noise (and let's face it, bagpipes can manage some pretty horrendous noises on their own).

Not according to Granny Nothing, of course. "Listen to that. The boy's a proditchy."

The Singhs were just back from seeing Nanny Sue off on her much-needed holiday. A two-week cruise. Fourteen days at sea, complete rest and relaxation. "Just what the poor girl needs," Mrs Singh said. They showed us the photograph they had taken of Nanny Sue as the ship sailed off into the sunset.

Her hair was standing on end and she looked as if she was screaming.

"You can see she needs a holiday, poor dear," Mrs Singh said.

Of course, they hadn't seen what we had. Sticking out of Nanny Sue's bag, arms outstretched towards her, was the mummy doll.

No wonder she was screaming. Two weeks at sea, just her and Inkibah the mummy. Revenge is sweet.

Ewen could hardly speak. "But we buried it, Steph. How did it get in her bag?"

I couldn't answer that. But I know there has to be a perfectly logical reason.

Hasn't there?

Granny Nothing looked at the photo and winked. "I dare say when I get Inkibah back in my case I can keep him there. As long as she behaves herself."

Then she laughed so much Thomas toppled out of his pouch. She caught him with one pink-gloved hand and stuffed him back in. "That's my boy," she said.

When it came time for Estelle to throw her bouquet I have never seen such an ungainly scuffle. It was embarrassing. The bouquet sailed up into the air, and suddenly, Mrs Scoular was jumping for it. Polly was leaping for it. But it was Granny Nothing who caught it, deftly, with one hand. "Och, would you believe this?" she said, sweetly. "Maybe it's time I had another man."

Baldy began to shake because Granny Nothing's eyes had turned on him.

When the Singhs started singing, Ewen and I took our wedding cake into the safety of the living room to eat it. Mrs Scoular was now chatting up Baldy (goodness, he's popular) and Polly was chasing Elvis, and it looked like Estelle was carrying Maurice over the threshold.

I switched on the TV. "Honestly, everyone's daft who lives here."

The news was just finishing. There had been some kind of hostage crisis, but it was over now. An undercover operation had rescued the hostages and they were safe.

"Turn it to another channel. I want something cheery on."

The other channel was showing some documentary programme about Nelson Mandela. There were pictures of his famous walk to freedom.

"This is rubbish as well!" Ewen said. "Are you sure there isn't a zombie film on?"

"This is history! This man is probably the greatest man alive, you nitwit. Watch and learn."

Nelson Mandela strode smiling through the crowds. Everyone was cheering. Women were trying to hug him. Men were patting him on the back. Granny Nothing was kissing him. Children were running. . .

Wait a minute!

"Did you see what I saw?" I said to Ewen.

"Did we see what we think we saw?" he said back.

"It couldn't be . . . could it?"

But with Granny Nothing . . . it possibly could.